Magick,
Straight Up

BARBARA DEVLIN

DEDICATION

For Mike.

CONTENTS

CHAPTER ONE

October 1, 2016

Big city doc Rafe Owen was a small town boy at heart. Born and raised in the asphalt jungle of Manhattan, he dreamed of the simple life in a blink-and-he-missed-it burb, which was why he jumped at the chance to temp in the Haven Harbor Regional Medical Center ER.

Fresh off the internship and specialty residency track, most new physicians jockeyed for high paying jobs in big name hospitals, while Rafe chose the not-so-glamorous life of a locum tenens, which meant he substituted for various professionals in the sort of places few wanted to work.

After he parked his car in the staff lot, he

locked the doors, pocketed his keys, and strolled to the grassy verge. Situated atop a bluff overlooking the Merrimack River, the hospital offered a great view of Haven Harbor, population thirteen thousand according to the sign, with its dense trees sporting fall foliage in autumn colors, manicured lawns, standard shaped courthouse square, and storybook charm.

As a light breeze kissed his face, he inhaled the clean, fresh air. "This just might be the home I've been searching for."

"Talking to yourself, young man?" Glancing over his shoulder, Rafe discovered a grey-haired stranger, wearing the traditional white coat of his trade. "We don't do much psychiatric work here, but I can recommend someone in Boston."

"Sorry if I scared you." Rafe chuckled and extended a hand in friendship. "Just admiring the landscape. You wouldn't know Josiah Adams, would you?"

"Depends on who's asking." The character smiled. "Are you a bill collector, a political pollster, or a process server?"

"No, sir." Rafe shook his head. "I'm Rafe Owen, the locum tenens relieving Dr. Adams."

"In that case, I would be Dr. Adams, but

you can call me Josiah, and it's nice to meet you, Dr. Owen." Josiah turned toward the ER. "I wasn't expecting you until tomorrow, but I can show you around, if you want."

"Just want to be ready to go, because I like to hit the ground running, and Rafe is fine." To the right, he noted the impressive helicopter pad. "Pretty sweet outfit you've got here. Don't know of many regional facilities equipped with such resources."

"We are blessed with generous supporters, and the entire medical campus underwent a substantial renovation last year." Dr. Adams pointed to the modern intake, reception, and waiting area. "We installed an efficient computer system, hired an expert IT team, and purchased state-of-the-art machines, all with the single intent of improving patient care."

"This is incredible." The chair rail moulding, pale yellow wall paint, and framed works of art, featuring posters and promotions from the town's signature event, the Witches Walk, gave the facility a hotel feel, and Rafe followed Josiah down the main corridor.

"The locker room and the lounge are to the left, and triage and the trauma unit are to the right." Despite his age, Josiah kept a quick pace. "The round the clock pharmacy and the cafeteria are back here, along with the offices, and if you continue down the hall, you will enter the main hospital."

"You said there were some differences regarding my assignment." In the neat and unassuming room, Rafe dropped into one of the plush seats positioned before the cleanest, uncluttered desk he'd ever seen. "Would you like to review my duties, or should we wait until tomorrow?"

"Now is as good a time as any, I suppose." Josiah tugged off his glasses and rubbed his eyes. "Since this is a small operation, the usual hierarchy doesn't apply. I am the Chief of ER Medicine, which means I pretty much run the show, but I also work for a living. While you act in my position, you will be subject to a twenty-four hour callback, like everyone else in our department. Is that a problem?"

"Got it, and it's no problem." That was a polite way of saying Rafe's social life would take a hit, but he was okay with that. "Anything else?"

"You are eager, aren't you?" Scratching his chin, Josiah smiled. "I remember those days, but they've long since passed me by. If you play your cards right, I just might retire, and this job could be yours, permanently, if you wish." With a yawn, he stretched upright. "Why don't you run over to Human Resources, and fill out your paperwork. They'll need your photo identification to issue your credentials, since your references and résumé were verified during the hiring process, and then you'll be all set."

"Sounds intriguing, and I'm interested, so we'll see how it goes this month." Rafe stood. "I've got to grab the keys to my rental and get unpacked, but then I'll be looking for food. Any recommendation on where I can get a cool drink and something decent to eat?"

"Do you travel much, aside from your work?" Josiah scooted from his worn, leather high-back chair, rounded the desk, and slapped Rafe on the shoulder. "Have any family?"

"My parents live in New York." Rafe shrugged. "Otherwise, it's just me."

"Sounds lonely." Folding his arms, Josiah furrowed his brow. "The Old Haven Mill Tavern, on Mill Street, has cold beer on tap, the best burgers on the East Coast, if not the US, and the Eye of Newt is my personal favorite. Ask for George, and see if the most famous bartender in Haven Harbor can guess your drink."

"Fascinating." Rafe nodded. "I'll give it a try."

Less than an hour after arriving, he figured out why tourism ads boldly declared *History is Witchstory in Haven Harbor,* because, like the ER, the walls in the hospital were decorated with framed posters from the famed Witches Walk charity event that took place annually, at the full moon in September, for the last eleven years. Maybe he'd find a sexy witch to keep him warm on cold nights.

After completing the typical BS associated with a new job, he returned to his car, opened the sunroof, and put down the windows. Veering right, he drove east on River Road until he came upon a row of Craftsman style homes some five minutes from work.

Just as the rental agent explained, two presented a perfectly matched set, if mirrored opposites, with taupe siding, burgundy shutters, and white trim. In the mailbox, he located the key, collected his bags, unlocked the door that boasted a dentil shelf and stained glass inserts, and stepped inside a slice of heaven.

With polished oak floors, matched wainscoting, cased windows, and earth toned paint, the old but restored and updated house included overstuffed furnishings and worn antiques. Granite, subway tile, a butcher block topped island, and a huge, apron-front sink complimented the stainless steel appliances in the kitchen. In what Rafe suspected was once a closet he found a powder room. Upstairs, he discovered a large bathroom and two bedrooms.

Since the front space contained a big desk and a smaller queen-sized bed, he decided to use that as a home office, and there he deposited his laptop. In the back, he unpacked his clothes and stashed his supply of condoms in the nightstand. Hey, a guy could hope. As he situated his personal items in the old, inset medicine cabinet, his stomach growled.

"Believe me, I hear you." After washing his face and brushing his teeth, he changed into a clean shirt, combed his hair, and headed out for the evening.

To get his bearings, he punched in the name of the tavern into his maps app and realized he wasn't that far from anything in Haven Harbor. In his car, he backed from the driveway, continued east on River Road, and crossed the bridge over Cascade Run River. Just past the park, at Birch Street, he hung a left. A few blocks north, he veered west on Mill Street, located the tavern, pulled into a spot at the curb, locked the doors, and followed a couple with four kids into the place.

Eighties music blared in the background of the restaurant, which featured a haunted mill motif that reminded him of his grandfather's barn in upstate New York. Most of the tables were occupied, and an army of servers, wearing shirts declaring a mix of odd sayings, such as *Get Your Spell On*, *Have You Kissed a Witch Today*, and *Save a Horse, Ride a Broom*, carried trays heaped with food.

"Can I help you, sir?" A young hostess checked her seating chart. "Booth for one, or will someone be joining you?"

"Can I eat in the bar?" Rafe glanced at the quieter side of the busy establishment. "And is George here?"

"Yes, sir. We serve the full menu in the bar." She nodded once. "And the boss works every day."

"Thanks." Three pool tables, each occupied, sat along the left wall, smaller tables framed an old, parquet dance floor, and what had to be the last mirror ball in existence dangled from the ceiling. A dated big-screen television loomed to the right, and a setup reminiscent of the Wild West ran the length of the back. In search of a little peace and quiet, he chose an empty stool at one end.

"Are you freaking kidding me?" On the floor, bent forward, with her ass in the air— ass perfection, to be accurate, his next temporary girlfriend reached beneath a cooler. "Gotcha."

Dusting off her tight-fitting jeans, the brunette stood upright, revealing a curvy figure and some great breasts. After grabbing a towel, she wiped what turned out to be a gold hoop earring, which she returned to its rightful place. In seconds, Rafe catalogued a series of examinations he planned to enjoy, involving his tongue, starting with that ear and traveling to her little toe.

As if on cue, she came alert, stared at him, and blushed. "Hello."

"Hi." What a mouth, and with those plump lips, he'd bet she gave great oral. Damn, he was horny. "I'm looking for George."

"Oh?" Although no one placed an order, she grabbed a tumbler and a shaker. "Mary-George McBride is my name, but everyone calls me George." In about a minute, she set a drink before him. "Vodka Collins with a twist. Do you prefer mustard or mayo on your Eye of Newt burger?"

"How did you know that's what I wanted?"

Surprised by her accuracy, he opened and closed his mouth. It had to be a trick. "Did Josiah Adams tell you he recommended the tavern?"

"Lucky guess." With a coy side-glance, she shrugged. "You're new here. How do you know Josiah?"

"I'm subbing for him at the hospital, while he goes on vacation." That revelation ought to change her attitude, and he expected she'd ask his name.

"That's nice." At the other end of the bar, George waved to an elderly gentleman. As she walked away, she peered over her shoulder. "If you need anything else, just let me know."

~

Hot sex wrapped in six feet of muscles, with the face of a Greek god, just the way George liked her men. Except he knew it. Just once, she'd like to meet a tourist or a visitor who wanted more than a free pass between her legs—or her ass, as the latest would-be Romeo indicated in his thoughts.

As a lifelong native of Haven Harbor, and a resident witch, she had been blessed, or cursed, with the claircognizance of desire, or what most people referred to as a gut hunch, only hers was uniquely tuned to wants. Yes, witches existed, as the town proclaimed with pride, but most folks figured the tongue-in-cheek approach was just a gimmick for advertising purposes, because no one possessed the ability to levitate cars or control other people.

And while most lore painted witches as broom riding, black pointy hat wearing, frizzy haired hags with nose warts, the truth was witches looked just like everyone else. Their powers, originating from birth, revolved around more harmless abilities, such as mediumship, telekinesis, clairvoyance, and prescience, although every now and then someone developed lycanthropy or another rare gift. Nothing out of the ordinary. Still, no one had anything to fear, as the Haven Harbor witches presented no threat.

"Okay, George." Bo Stanton, a retired cop living on a fixed income, tapped his chin peppered with grey and black stubble and arched a brow. Every night, he enacted the same routine, and she adored him. "What am I thinking?"

"You want the Witch's Hemlock IPA." She grabbed a pint glass.

"Hot dog, she got it." A widower, Bo slapped his thighs, and the crowd cheered. "George does it again."

"Here you go, Bo." Drawing on her particular skill, she tuned into his overwhelming hunger and clenched her gut. "Hey, I made a huge mistake and thawed too much beef for the dinner rush, and I'd sure hate for it to go to waste. If I ask Tony to fix you a plate, on the house, would you care to eat? You'd be doing me a big favor."

"Well, I don't know." He licked his lips.

"What if I throw in some fries, and maybe a slice of apple pie with a scoop of my homemade vanilla bean ice cream?" She punched in the order on the computer touchscreen. "I'd sure appreciate it, Bo."

"Since you put it that way, you're on, little lady." When she folded a cloth napkin into a triangle and draped it on the bar, as a makeshift placemat, he sat up straight and smoothed the edges. Leaning forward, Bo whispered, "Did you really goof?"

"I did." Covering his hand with hers, she squeezed his fingers. "You're my best customer, and I have to keep you coming back."

"You know, if I was twenty years younger, I'd marry you." Bo winked.

"Oh, talk like that could sweep a girl off her feet." Laughing, she noticed Casanova flagging her and groaned. "Be right back."

Struggling to muster a smile, she returned to her obnoxious guest, whose naughty urges brought a flush to her face, and she snagged her ice water from the counter. As before, his inner dialogue focused on seduction, and she swallowed the urge to slap him. "Your food should be out, any minute."

"I need another drink." He scooted the empty tumbler to the edge of the bar. "What do you recommend?"

The doctor seriously needed to get laid, but she couldn't serve that in a glass. To delay, so she could sense his craving, she prepared a similar dining setup. Finally, she sifted through the various wants, which exercised her mind, and pinned his preference. "You want an old-fashioned, but with brandy instead of whiskey."

"That's incredible." With elbows propped on the ledge, he cradled his chin in his palms and gawked, and she made a point to ignore him. "The name is Rafe Owen, in case you're interested. My friends call me Rafe, and I'd like to be your friend, if you let me."

"Really?" Assailed by a host of new and shocking suggestions, which wreaked havoc on her senses, she rolled her eyes. "Does that ever work?"

"You want the truth?" Rafe grinned. "All

the time."

Just then, a waitress delivered his food, and the poor girl almost tripped when he thanked her.

"That is so not right." Folding her arms, she stiffened her spine. "Katie just set women back a hundred years."

Don Juan burst into laughter.

"In her defense, she just turned twenty-one." In response to his silent broadcast, George fetched a bottle of ketchup. "Can I get you anything else?"

"You could join me." Valentino inclined his head, and a collective female sigh declared not everyone found him obnoxious. If only they could sense his desires. "My treat."

"No, thanks." She wiped down the cutting board and washed a paring knife, as he again obsessed over her boobs.

"How about I buy you a drink." And now he just wanted to get into her undies.

Of course, she had a justifiable but nice reason to reject his offer. "No can do, unless I want to lose my liquor license."

"Ah, okay." He narrowed his stare. "Did I say something to offend you?"

No, but he *thought* something offensive. "I'm sorry?"

"We seem to have started on the wrong

foot. Can we try again?" He extended a hand, and she accepted the gesture but flinched when he kissed her knuckles. To her surprise, he abandoned the dirty talk in his mind. "My name is Rafe Owen, and I'm the new doctor in town."

"And I'm Mary-George McBride, the owner and head bartender of the Old Haven Mill Tavern." In the spirit of second chances, she curtseyed. "Welcome, Rafe."

"Are you Haven Harbor, born and raised?" Hefting the burger, he took a massive bite and hummed.

"I'll take that as a good sign." From a shelf, she grabbed a short stack of paper napkins and set them to his right. "And I've lived here, forever."

"This is the best burger I've ever tasted." In a flash, she pulled a clean glass from the washer and filled it with ice and water. "Okay, you're starting to scare me."

"I can take it back." She laughed at his owlish expression and focused on his reaction. There was more to him than the chiseled profile, expensive clothing, and god-awful inclinations, and that was the Rafe she'd like to know better, but she doubted he'd let her get close enough.

Not quite an audible voice or as sharp as a

bodily motion, her gift manifested itself as an energy, for lack of a better term, that had taken her years to decipher and comprehend. Neither tangible nor elusive, her mystical perceptions could inspire a variety of reactions, both physical and emotional, and she was powerless to stop it. Dynamic and constantly evolving, the unique ability spoke to her on some spiritual level that defied reason, and there was no way to avoid it. She couldn't just put her hands over her ears and silence it, though she often tried as a young girl.

"So what do you do for fun around here?" Given his question, she braced for a new assault, and he didn't disappoint her. Couldn't he think of something original?

"I volunteer at the senior citizen's center." That ought to cool his jets.

"Wow, that's pretty wild." Ah, she sparked his curiosity. "Maybe you should tone it down a bit."

In that instant, she noted Rafe had cleaned his plate. "Dessert?"

"What do you have to tempt me?" Oh, no. Again with the ass. She almost felt sorry for him.

"I don't think we serve that here." It was a shame, really, because he'd been blessed with a killer combination. Pale blue eyes and raven hair commanded attention, and despite his coarse musings, she could appreciate his beauty.

"That's too bad." When she collected his dishes, he leaned forward. "Let me take you to dinner, you name the date, time, and place."

He was nothing if not persistent, and it was his misfortune that George was equally stubborn. "Is it really that easy?"

"Oh, it's really that easy." His dimpled smile, alone, melted her panties, if she was honest with herself. "You see I have a surefire line. Want to hear it?"

Okay, so there was a twisted charm about him. "I'm all ears."

"I've got roughly four million in the bank, I'm a doctor, and I'm single." Not once did he blink.

Whereas she almost choked on his bold statement. "That's it?"

Unabashed, he shrugged. "You'd be amazed."

"That doesn't speak well of my sex." Per his desire, she printed the bill and handed it to him.

"What can I say?" He shrugged, as he pulled his wallet from his back pocket. "And who am I to deny a woman in need?"

"How benevolent." She'd just bet he'd satisfied a slew of ladies, and she had no intention of serving as the next notch in his bedpost.

"So what about our evening?" After counting a few bills, Rafe put the cash on the counter, along with a business card, and stood. "That's my cell, and you can call whenever you want. I meant what I said, so it's your choice. Anything you want."

"Maybe one day, if you're sincere, I'll take you up on your offer." With a clean rag, George wiped the bar. When he turned to leave, she couldn't resist adding, "Until then, I like your ass, too."

CHAPTER TWO

The blaring buzzer signaled six o'clock, and Rafe stretched long as he turned off the alarm. Yawning, he kicked aside the covers and rolled out of bed. Although he wasn't due at the hospital until eight, he enjoyed the morning hours, so he began every day with a hot shower, his favorite, custom coffee blend, a hearty breakfast, and the local newspaper.

After bathing, he brushed his teeth, dried his hair, dressed, and headed downstairs. The auto-timer on the machine ensured his java was waiting when he strolled into the kitchen, and he poured himself a steaming mug before he pulled a skillet from the cupboard. Just as he collected the eggs from the fridge, a flirty little hum caught his attention, and he glanced out the window and discovered a woman dressed in sweats, with her long brown hair in a ponytail, on her hands and knees, pulling a stray weed from a flowerbed.

"I'd know that ass anywhere." Laughing, he shook his head and nabbed his cup of joe. At the side entry, he quietly flipped the bolt and yanked open the door. "Good morning, George."

Emitting a shriek, the fascinating bartender jumped and peered over her shoulder. "What are you doing here?"

"It appears I'm your new next-door neighbor." Gazing at the sky, a watercolor of blue and pink hues, he savored the fresh air. "You always do yard work at the crack of dawn?"

"You're my new tenant?" Standing upright, she tugged off her gloves and tucked a stray tendril behind her ear. "And I have to take care of lawn maintenance now, because this is Monday, which is when the community hosts the potluck lunch at the Haven Harbor senior citizens center, on Willow Street, so I need to cook a couple of casseroles and a dessert, prior to opening the tavern for the noon rush."

"Wait a minute. You're my landlord?" He revisited their conversation and realized she wasn't joking. She really volunteered, and

Rafe found her far more intriguing in that moment. Hot body aside, George had spirit, and he wanted to know her beyond the physical sense. "I don't remember seeing your name on the contract."

"So it seems." A brisk wind buffeted her, and she turned into the breeze. "My agent handles the listing, the rental agreement, and the background check."

"Hey, do you want to come inside for a bit?" He held high the mug to tempt her, and he hoped she didn't reject him, because he suspected she was something special. "The host provides eggs, bacon, and toast."

"Well, I have a lot to do, which is why I got an early start." For a few seconds, she just stared at him, and he wished he knew what she was thinking. "But I have to eat, and I'd enjoy the company, if you're sure it's not too much trouble."

"Pretty lady, you're never trouble." As he ushered her inside, he almost knocked her over when she halted.

"Whoa." She lifted her chin and inhaled. "What is that heavenly aroma?"

"Coffee." Firing up the burner, he chuckled. "My propriety mix, and you can help yourself, while I whip up some grub. How do you like your eggs?"

"Oh, I'm not picky." Since the house was hers, it didn't surprise him that she located a mug, with ease. "Sunny side up is fine with me. Any chance you have some of those sickeningly sweet cinnamon rolls that come in a can? I love those things."

"Hey, that's my favorite, too." He dropped a pat of butter in the pan, adjusted the flame to low, and draped several strips of bacon into a second skillet. "And no cinnamon rolls, but thanks for the tip."

"Imagine that." There was something cryptic in her tone, reminiscent of the ass comment she made when he was leaving the tavern, but he brushed it off. It was as though she read his mind. Of course, that was impossible, because if she had, she'd have slapped him.

"Tell me something." With care, Rafe cracked four eggs. "Did you really make a mistake last night, or do you often feed Bo for free?"

"Please, don't say anything to him." The anxiety in her expression broadcast her genuine concern for the old codger, as she popped the bread in the toaster. It was crazy, how well she anticipated his every need, because he'd just met her, yet they made a great team. "He barely survives on a police officer's pension, after Mabel's death from cancer. Despite numerous offers of help through the hospital's charity fund, and from his daughter, he insists on paying his wife's exorbitant bills, so I do what I can on the sly."

"That's very generous of you, and your secret is safe with me." Okay, while she had magnificent curves, her mind and altruistic nature were her best assets, and he had seriously underestimated her worth. "But you might consider his overall health and cholesterol levels, and offer a grilled chicken breast sandwich, with a fresh salad, instead of a burger and fries. At his age, he needs to watch his diet."

"What a great idea." From a shelf, she retrieved two placemats and set the table. "I'll give Tony a list of wholesome and nutritious options for future reference, so he can feed Bo when I'm not there."

"Is he the inspiration for your work at the senior citizens center?" All right, George was a keeper, the sort of woman who brought out the worst in a man—his personal code of ethics, and she piqued his interest as well as Mr. Happy. "Or do you come by it honestly?"

"I wish I could take credit for it, but I'm continuing the work my parents started."

True to character, she held their plates, as Rafe dished the fare. "They died four years ago, in a car accident on ninety-five. The tavern was our family business, and I assumed control after I earned a degree in business." After depositing their meal on the table, she fetched the silverware, and he pulled out her chair. "My dad held an annual benefit to support the center, and my mother supervised the day lounge. The least I can do is maintain the tradition."

"I'm sorry about your folks." Whatever it took, he would win a date with the brown-eyed goddess, because he had to exist in her world, if only for a month. "Any brothers or sisters?"

"A younger brother, and he's at school in Boston." To his utter amazement, she buttered his toast just as he preferred it, and he simply couldn't explain her uncanny ability to guess his every desire. "When Russell Lee comes home on the weekends, he stays with our grandmother, in town."

The rest of the meal passed in quiet, as he studied his guest. Despite his best efforts to identify what she possessed that drew him to her, she stumped him. There was something about the beautiful bartender, yet there was a particular aspect about which he was certain.

"You have a good heart, George."

"Is that an official diagnosis, Dr. Owen?" Blushing, she averted her stare. Yep, she was humble, too. "Or an opinion?"

Without prompt, she stacked the empty plates, collected the silverware, and carried everything to the sink.

"An observation." A racy remark danced on the tip of his tongue, but he kept it to himself, because he genuinely liked her, and he'd find a way to make her see past his slick New York exterior. "At the risk of being rude, I'm going to have to ask you to leave, because I have to get to the hospital."

"No problem." After loading the last item in the dishwasher, she wiped her hands on a towel. Once again, her cheeks flushed red, and she bit her lip. Damn, she was hot. "Hey, doc, what time does your shift end?"

"Seven, at the latest." Dare he hold his breath? "Why?"

"I'm running a special at the tavern, tonight." Ah, she favored him with a hint of a smile, and his prospects improved. "Grilled chicken sandwich, lettuce, tomato, red onion, and avocado, on a whole wheat bun, with a side salad. If you're interested, I'll take my break and join you when you arrive."

"Honey, you don't have to ask me twice."

~

What the hell had she been thinking?

In the bathroom, George stared at her reflection in the mirror, brushed her mane, and freshened her lipstick. "What am I doing? I don't wear makeup to work."

With a huff, she tossed the tube into her purse and yanked the zipper shut. Smoothing the front of her form-fitting blouse, she turned left and then right, before groaning.

Yes, she'd worn nice clothes—girl clothes, she'd styled her hair, and she'd painted her face for her appointment with the cute doc, and he didn't show. It was seven-thirty, and she was starved, but there she lingered, clinging to hope with a futile touchup.

"I should have known better, based on his not-so-nice thoughts, last night." Of course, it was the authentic sincerity Rafe unwittingly relayed over breakfast that swayed her in his favor. In fact, the more time she spent in his company, she realized he tucked away secrets only he knew, and she hoped he would share them with her. "He's probably sitting at home, laughing at me, right now."

Well, she couldn't hide forever, so she wiped a stray tear and blew her nose. With one more check of her appearance, she returned to the bar and found her man, dressed in dark jeans and a plaid button-down, with his back to her, looming in the center of the room. When he scanned the area, he spied her and smiled, and she sensed enormous relief—his and hers.

"George, I'm so sorry I'm late, but the ER was a mess. We had a broken leg that needed to be set, a kid with a head injury, a police officer who cut his palm and required sutures, and a lady involved in a fender bender, and I couldn't leave. Plus, I didn't have your number, so I called the tavern, but the line was busy." Unknowingly, Rafe showered her in invisible but nonetheless potent regret that begged forgiveness, and she couldn't resist him. Then he blinked. "Wow. You look amazing. If I crawl on my knees, will you forgive me?"

"Done." The anxiety vanished, as she waved to Danny, one of her staff bartenders, and he punched in her ticket. In preparation for their first date, she preordered everything, so she had only to signal her team, and dinner would arrive soon. "Can I get you a drink?"

"I'm exhausted, and I have an early meeting, so I better take it easy." He opened his mouth but clamped it shut and narrowed his stare. Oh, he was in a playful mood, and she was in mood to play. "What do I want?"

Tapping her chin, she pretended to give the query ample consideration. "Iced tea with extra lemon, coming right up, sir."

"Hot dog, George does it again." In good sport, Rafe saluted Bo, who nodded an acknowledgement from his usual perch.

As she ambled to the counter, Dr. Owen's admiration of her ass, which manifested as a powerful hunger mixed with searing heat, didn't escape her notice, but his was more an expression of appreciation and gratitude, as opposed to his previous thoughts, which she wouldn't repeat even in her mind. In seconds, she filled a glass, tossed in a few plump, juicy wedges, and returned to her guest.

A rush of excitement overtook her, and she couldn't help but laugh. "So you're happy to see me?"

"I've been waiting for this all day. Hell, I was so preoccupied, as I treated an ingrown toenail, I walked into a closed door." With an elbow propped on the table, he smiled, and the energy he emitted intensified. "Now tell me the secret to your trick. How do you guess what people want, with such accuracy, because you nailed it?"

And Rafe's desire screamed he wanted to nail her.

"Oh, it's actually pretty simple." Struggling

to manage the force of his enthusiasm, which grew with every passing minute, George fidgeted in her stool, but deep down inside, where she was always honest with herself, she had to admit she wanted him, too. Still, it was way too soon to trust him with the truth of her gift. "Think of it as a suggestion. I read body language, picking up clues from the individual."

"Come on." He arched a brow. "I've been here just over twenty-four hours, and you haven't missed, yet."

"Two specials with a side salad and low-cal vinaigrette. Don't know why you bother." Wrinkling his nose, Tony lowered a tray to serve the meal, and she sighed in relief, uttering silent thanks for the interruption. "Sure you don't want an order of fries or some artery clogging mayo?"

"That'll be all, Tony." Oh, she was never going to hear the end of it.

"Then you two lovebirds enjoy." Tony grinned. Her cook was so dead.

Time to change the subject.

"You know, during our exchanges, you've never told me where you're from." After unrolling her silverware, she cut her sandwich in half. A tidal wave of unmistakable longing had her hands shaking, as she took a bite.

"I was born and raised in Manhattan." George detected a hint of sadness in Rafe's voice. "My father is a renowned neurosurgeon, and my mother is a New York socialite. Beyond that, there's not much to share."

"Any brothers or sisters?" To distract herself from his overwhelming yearning for something she couldn't quite identify, she scooted a cherry tomato about her plate.

"Nope." And that was his response. No jokes. No frisky side commentary from his inner psyche. Just a void.

"Aside from the job at the hospital, what brings you to Haven Harbor?" In search of anything to divert her from the pain building in her gut, she made a mental note to have Tony add some of his special Cajun spices to the chicken breast, because it could use a kick. "I'd think our little town would be too boring for a city boy." She shrugged. "There's no first-class symphony, Broadway theatre, or Yankees. Instead, we have the community jam session, made up of local musicians, every Thursday night at the library, the Haven Harbor Opera House, which produces small plays and musicals, and the Ospreys of Haven Harbor High School."

"I'll take that, any day of the week, along

with the clean air, the large yards, the quirky hangouts where everyone knows your name, and the beautiful bartender who knows just what I want to drink." But Rafe neglected to mention the family he desired, above all else, and it was that want that struck her as a punch in the stomach, and she doubled over in agony. "Hey, are you okay?"

"I'm fine." When he covered her hand with his, comforting warmth unfurled and spread, traveling the length of her arm, soothing her frazzled nerves and erasing the tension. Rafe hid so much from the world, but he couldn't conceal anything from George, and she sensed the secrets he kept tucked in his heart. Twining her fingers in his, she smiled. "Really, it's nothing. I haven't eaten since breakfast. The dishwasher backed up and flooded the kitchen, and the plumber didn't arrive until four, which was when we needed to prep for the dinner rush."

"Sounds like we both had a rough day." With his thumb, he drew circles on her palm. "But this makes it all worthwhile. So when can I take you out on a real date? You know, I pick you up at your place, we have dinner at an expensive restaurant, and maybe go to a movie." Then he'd violate her every way possible.

"Finish your sandwich, before it gets cold." George broke their physical connection and glanced at her watch, because she wasn't sure how to answer him. Part of her wanted to accept his offer, and the other half of her wanted to run. "And I have to get back to work."

"You can't take the rest of the night off?" The lopsided grin tempted her, especially when Rafe inclined his head. How could anyone turn him down? "I'll take you anywhere you want to go, just name it."

"That would leave my employees short-staffed, and I'd never do that." Yet she considered his offer, if only to learn more about him. A loud crash echoed through the bar, followed by thunderous applause, and George spotted a woeful waitress near the jukebox. Charging the fore, she motioned to the busboy. "Charlie, fetch the broom, the mop, and the bucket, on the double, please."

"I'm so sorry, George." Cindy, one of Russell Lee's old high school friends, shuffled her feet. Too poor to attend college, and unable to get a scholarship, she remained in Haven Harbor, while most of her classmates embarked on the next phase of their lives. "I cleared three tables, including a six-top, and I thought I could balance everything, but the stack of plates shifted. Should have waited for Charlie."

"Are you okay?" George gathered several large shards of broken porcelain and scooped a pile of leftover food. "Because that's all that matters."

"I'm fine." Cindy shrugged. "Just a bruised ego."

"George, go back to your dinner date." Tony wheeled in the large janitorial trolley, equipped with a wringer. "Wait—let me say that again. Go back to your dinner date, because we know that doesn't happen every day."

"Thanks, a lot, Tony." She rolled her eyes. When Rafe burst into laughter behind her, she flinched. As she faced the hot doc, she sighed in frustration. "Pretend you didn't hear that."

"Hear what?" His smirk declared otherwise, and he cast an expression of mock contrition when she narrowed her gaze. "Look, we're pretty much done for tonight, but I want to know when I can see you again."

"Oh, lord, my prayers have been answered." Peering at the ceiling, Tony clutched his fist to his chest. "He's willing to risk a second tour of duty. You better grab him, fast, George, before he gets away.

You're not getting any younger."

"Come with me." With a death grip on Rafe's wrist, she dragged him to the exit. "I'll walk you out."

"Wait." He drew her to a halt. "I have to pay the check."

"I got it." To her embarrassment, the hostess snorted and pretended to be busy, as George pulled Rafe outside and into the brisk night air.

"Now you have to let me buy you dinner." At the curb, he turned, yanked hard, and hauled her into his arms. Before she could protest, he covered her mouth with his.

Last winter, at a coven meeting, she sat too close to the hearth, and the fire singed her jeans, resulting in a mild burn, sort of like a sunburn, to her ass, and she couldn't sit comfortably for a month. The searing heat of Rafe's kiss, which touched her everywhere, coupled with his desire, which invested her senses, was a thousand times hotter and way more jolting than her clumsy goof, and when he teased her tongue with his, she damn near melted against him.

Imaginary stars burst overhead, delicious shivers tap-danced along her spine, in her brain Pavarotti's rendition of Puccini's singular tenor aria "Nessun Dorma," from the opera *Turandot*, reached its signature crescendo, and her knees buckled.

Then he broke free and set her on her heels. "That's how you end a great date, in case you forgot."

"Very funny." With trembling fingers, she caressed her bottom lip.

"Breakfast, tomorrow, at my place. I'll leave the door unlocked." He strolled to the driver's side of a sleek black Mercedes. "Say, six-thirty? I've got eggs, bacon…and cinnamon rolls."

What? It was only that morning she shared her addiction to the sweet treats. "You didn't."

"I did." With a shameless grin, he glanced over the roof of his car. "Goodnight, George, and thanks for the meal."

"Sweet dreams, Rafe, and you're welcome." Okay, she wanted him—bad. "See you in the AM."

CHAPTER THREE

A glance at the clock on the wall made it clear Rafe wasn't going to make his date with George, and he gritted his teeth, as he stitched the last suture on the left knee of a young boy who took a nasty fall on the playground, during an afterschool game of kickball at Haven Harbor Elementary. After assessing his handiwork, he stripped off his rubber gloves and tossed them in the trash.

"Okay, Timmy, we're all done, and you are one tough little guy." Supporting the child's neck, Rafe helped his patient sit upright. "But no kickball until your doctor removes the stitches." To Timmy's mother, Rafe said, "Follow up with your primary care physician, tomorrow, keep the area clean and dry, and limit his activities for the next couple of days."

"Thank you, so much, Dr. Owen." She wagged a finger at her son. "Do you hear that? And no skateboarding, either."

In response, Timmy howled in protest.

"I'll send in the nurse with discharge instructions, once I complete and sign the chart." Rafe swept aside the privacy curtain and walked into the hall. At the nurse's station, he commandeered a terminal and typed in his diagnosis, treatment, and further recommendations for recovery, with lightning speed.

"You're moving like you've got the devil on your tail." Minnie Terwilliger, the feisty, grey-haired, most senior employee in the ER, and the resident comedian, hugged her belly and laughed. "What's up, doc? You got a private appointment with that sweet Mary-George McBride?"

"What makes you think that?" Ah, yes. The small town curse, where everyone knew his business. Glancing at his phone, he discovered a text from the lady in question.

George: Can't wait till tonight. BTW, those cinnamon rolls are making me fat. You might not appreciate that when you finally see me naked, which could be sooner than you realize...

The second message left him cursing under

his breath.

George: I bought something lacy for our night out. You might reflect on that while we're at the library.

Damn. He was going to get lucky, and he had to bail, when he'd actively pursued the bartender.

For the past three mornings, they'd come together at dawn to start their day in each other's company, and in honor of their date, he surprised her with a dozen roses. To his infinite gratitude, the luscious tavern owner thanked him by planting her gorgeous round ass in his lap and showering his face in kisses. He was so hard that, after she departed for work, he had to jack off before speeding to the hospital. Now he had to disappoint her, as well as himself, which hurt far more than he anticipated, so he tapped a quick response and braced for impact.

Rafe: Hey, babe. I'd rather have a tarantula lay eggs in my ear than cancel on you, but we're swamped, and I can't leave. But I'd crawl on all fours, buck-ass nude, across a trail of broken glass, for a glimpse of your body, in any shape. Rain check? Please?

"Paging Dr. Owen." Minnie slapped a thigh and shook her head. "Did you hear what I just said?"

"Huh?" Blinking, he came alert, and Minnie frowned. "What was that?"

"Pay attention, doc, because I don't often repeat myself." Narrowing her stare, Minnie scanned the intake screen. "You've got one in x-ray, and we're waiting on the results of the CAT scan of the accident victim in T-2."

"I'm on it." When his phone buzzed, he unlocked the display.

George: Understand. Don't work too hard.

Rafe: Breakfast, tomorrow? Usual time?

George: I'll think about it.

Uh-oh.

Rafe: I'm groveling. Pretty please, with a hot, fresh cinnamon roll on top?

George: You'll probably be tired from work.

Rafe: Never too tired for you. I'll give you all the extra cream cheese icing.

Silence.

Rafe: Come on, babe. Let me make it up to you.

Nada.

Did his phone go dead?

Rafe: I'd call and plead my case, but I'm standing in the hall of a packed ER, and I don't want to cry in front of my patients.

George: Really, it's okay. Get some rest, doc.

Well, hell. If only he could tell her how much he wanted to spend time with her. If only she knew how he looked forward to their mornings, because he enjoyed talking to her.

Yes, that was a new experience for him,

because conversation had never rated on his list of requirements when it came to girlfriends, but when it came to George, he realized he'd grossly underestimated meaningful discussions with women. While he still wanted in her panties, it was her mind and her generous spirit that drew him to her. Hopefully, he hadn't just destroyed the progress he'd made in the last few days.

After pocketing his phone, he returned to work, pissed that he'd ruined their evening and vowing to make it right. Perhaps a serious investment in The Enchanted Florist would aid his cause.

The hours ticked past in a haze of complaints, some serious, others less so. He admitted a nice old lady in the waning moments of life, sent home a young man suffering nothing more than a stomachache from the overconsumption of candy, and treated a bloody nose from what was supposed to have been a touch football game. When an ambulance pulled onto the ramp, Rafe exhaled and rubbed the back of his neck.

"Dr. Owen, you can go home." Minnie adjusted her glasses and studied her clipboard. While he was chief of the ER, he quickly figured out she was the queen. "Dr. Samuels said he'd take the next case, because he's got third shift."

"Then I'm out of here." Without even stopping to shed his white coat, he pumped a palm full of sanitizing gel, cleaned his hands, walked through the main entrance, and broke into a sprint when he reached the parking lot. In seconds, he unlocked his car and jumped behind the wheel. The clock in the dashboard marked the hour as nine-thirty, and he revved the engine and raced the five minutes down River Road to home and George.

To his unimaginable disappointment and frustration, when he parked in the driveway, her front windows were dark, and her porch light was off. Still, he found himself at her door with his finger just an inch from the bell, but he paused.

"Damn, George, I really wanted to see you tonight." Everything inside him wanted to bang his fist until she appeared, to sweep her off her feet and carry her to his bed, but he retreated. "If I remember correctly, you're working a double tomorrow, so I shouldn't disturb you."

Tired, defeated, and hungry, Rafe retraced his steps and dragged into his living room. After stripping free of his white coat, which he flung on the floor, he collapsed on the couch, stared at the ceiling, and laughed when his stomach growled.

Rolling onto his side, he stretched his legs over the edge of the well-worn sofa, sat upright, and stood. With a yawn, he stumbled into the kitchen, opened the fridge, and considered his choices, which were few, as the extent of his grocery shopping centered on breakfast with George. Just as he reached for a wedge of cheddar cheese, someone knocked at the side door.

When he peered through the blind, he smiled, disengaged the bolt, and yanked on the knob. "Beautiful lady, you must've read my mind."

"Fancy that." Lugging a shopping bag, George bit her bottom lip and pushed past him. On the counter, she set a large covered bowl and a plate wrapped in tin foil. "I figured you might not have had a chance to eat, since you were busy, so I brought you some of my homemade chili and buttermilk cornbread. All you have to do is nuke it, and you're good to go." Clothed in her familiar tight jeans and a sweatshirt, she didn't notice he'd moved behind her until he rested his palms to her hips and turned her about to face him. "I wasn't planning to stay. I just wanted to make sure you had a hot meal."

In one swift move, he backed her against

the cabinets and kissed her.

Yea, she brought him a hot meal, just not the one she intended.

With a firm grasp of her round ass, he initiated a hell of a bump and grind, trying to calm his erection before he blew his wad, as he darted his tongue into her warm mouth and shuddered. When she unbuttoned his pants and shoved her hand down his boxers, he grabbed her wrist.

"Easy, babe." He clenched his gut. "I'm ready to bust."

"Is that so bad?" She licked his neck and sucked on his ear lobe. "I want you, but I'll go home, if you need to get to bed."

"Oh, we're going to bed, soon enough." None too gently, Rafe swept her shirt over her head and discovered a lacy black bra that hid nothing from him, and he pinched a pert nipple through the thin fabric. "Was this my surprise?"

George nodded. "There's matching undies, too."

"Now this I have to see." As much as he hated to do it, he parted from her. "Show me."

Ah, the blush made an achingly sweet return, as she kicked off her tennis shoes, tugged on her socks, and dropped her jeans.

"After the great breakfasts you've cooked for me, and the lovely mornings we've shared, I wanted to look pretty for you, and I wanted tonight to be special."

"Trust me, it will be. And you're beautiful, George." Then Rafe pounced.

Lifting the sultry bartender in his arms, he sat her atop the table. After removing her barely-there panties, he inched his pants to his knees, spread her thighs, positioned himself, flexed his spine, and thrust.

So began the most incredible night of his life.

A rhythmic thump played in unison with his movements, as he plowed into her, again and again. Driven by need, by sheer force of desire, he dug his fingers into her legs, and she scooted upright and wrapped her limbs about him. In seconds, he relocated to the floor.

Propped on his elbows, he took her, hard and fast, and counted her subtle moans uttered in unison with his frontal assault a reward for his efforts. An awkward contest commenced, as they wrestled for control of their heated exchange, but he maintained the advantage. They toppled a reading lamp, tipped over the coffee table, and when he withdrew from her body and stood, she shoved him into the overstuffed chair, straddled him, and rode him like a banshee, completely out of control.

At one point, he pinned her against a wall, and they started when they knocked loose a mirror, but even that didn't slow them for long. On the sofa, he tossed the throw pillows to the rug, situated her ankles on his shoulders, and resumed his siege, burying his flesh deep within hers. Although he wanted to draw out the moment, to linger, to take his time and create a memory to commemorate the milestone in their relationship, nothing could have prepared him for the strength of her hunger, when she gripped his ass and screamed. No, he couldn't resist her.

The power of her orgasm sent him soaring, higher and higher, until he came in a rush of vicious spasms that rendered him weak and gasping for air. Collapsing atop her, he groaned with each successive contraction, which seemed never-ending. At last, he caught his breath.

"Damn, I needed that." Lifting his head, Rafe grinned. "But I guess it's too late to worry about birth control."

"Just a little." Wiping the perspiration from her brow, George smiled. "Relax, because I'm on the pill." Then she cupped his cheek. "If you want, I can leave. I don't mind."

"Not a chance, and I'd mind." With care, he disengaged from her, bent his legs, kissed each breast, and pushed from the couch. "Right now, we're going to fix the chili and cornbread, because I'm starved, and then we're going to continue what we started here, until dawn."

~

The heavenly aroma of fresh baked cinnamon rolls teased her nose, and George stretched and opened her eyes. Then she panicked amid the unfamiliar surroundings. A series of rapid-fire memories, downright illicit, brought her alert, and she lurched upright. To her left, Rafe's side of the bed was empty, and she recalled his tender lovemaking, after he gently roused her from sleep, just a couple of hours ago, and smiled.

Stretching her arms overhead, she scooted to the edge of the mattress, stood, and winced. "Oh."

With aches and pains in muscles she didn't know she had, she moved slowly. Naked, she searched for her jeans and sweatshirt and recalled she'd left the items on the kitchen floor. A robe had been draped on the old footboard, and she shrugged into the warm garment. The fabric smelled like her handsome host, and visions of him looming above her flashed in her brain, and she hummed as she walked down the hall and into the bathroom.

On the counter, she found a new toothbrush, a tube of toothpaste, a bottle of mouthwash, a container of facial cleanser, and a cloth. The man thought of everything, and she adored him for it.

Awake and refreshed, she skipped downstairs and found her hot doc, barefooted and wearing nothing but sweatpants, pulling a pan of cinnamon rolls from the oven. Was there anything sexier in the world than a guy who cooked?

"Good morning, Rafe." Swallowing her hesitation, she remained rooted to the spot, as he approached and enfolded her in his arms.

"Hey, how'd you sleep?" A wave of lust touched her everywhere, as he pressed his lips to her forehead. Even after everything they'd done in the wee hours, he still wanted her. "And it's a great morning, George."

"Like a rock, once I actually got to rest." In a chair, he'd folded and stacked her clothes, and she peered at the table. Given what they did there, her cheeks burned.

"Don't worry." He nudged her nose with

his and kissed her. "I cleaned it with a bleach wipe before I placed the dishes."

"Coffee?" Uncomfortable for some reason she couldn't understand, she pulled free. Maybe it was because her emotions interfered with her ability to read him clearly. At the cabinet, she retrieved a couple of mugs and poured two cups of steaming java. Inhaling the incredible scent, she moaned. "I could get used to this."

"Okay." His undeniable desire shot to the fore, and she realized he spoke the truth. He wanted her there.

Meeting his gaze, she leaned against the counter. "How did this happen?"

"I have no idea, but I'm running with it." Then he shrugged. "Have to admit, I like having you in my bed. Or against the wall, on the floor, on the table, and on the sofa. And we still need to christen the shower, my car, and your house." He clucked his tongue. "I'm not picky, as long as I've got you."

"Do you mean that?" Of course, even as she uttered the words, his energy left her in no doubt of his sincerity, but could she trust him with her secret?

"George, I've thought a lot about us in a short span, and I can't make sense of anything." Holding the skillet, Rafe dished their eggs and bacon. "But I also know I don't want to question whatever we're doing." As he grabbed the pan of cinnamon rolls, he shook his head. "Take this for what it's worth, and don't panic, but I'm happy, and I can't remember the last time I said that about myself. Can we leave it at that for a while and see where this takes us?"

"Sure." The longing, the hunger for something to fill a seemingly endless void returned to his psyche, and she scooped a large bite of eggs as she deciphered his inner dialogue. At some point, she was going to have to reveal her unique gift and unusual life, but part of her feared his reaction and possible rejection, because mockery and abandonment often resulted from her candor with past boyfriends, and she didn't want to risk losing him. "What are you doing today? What's your schedule?"

"I'm working the second shift, because another doctor needed the evening off, so I might go back to bed." He waggled his brows. "Someone kept me up all night."

"And you *were* up all night." In fact, she'd never known any guy with so much stamina. In some respects, Rafe fucked like a machine, because he kept going and going and going. "I've got to open the tavern, but if I could, I'd soak in a hot bath."

"How's your ass?" Frowning, he reached for her hand and squeezed her fingers. "Why didn't you tell me you'd never gone there? I would've bought some lube and taken it slow, because I don't ever want to hurt you."

"I'm sore." Her cheeks went up in flames, and she bit her bottom lip as she revisited the shocking moment when he rolled her onto her belly, spread her legs, and took her butt from behind. "Real sore. And I didn't say anything because I knew you wanted it." Indeed, he'd wanted it bad, and she couldn't deny him.

"Baby, I'm not trying to embarrass you, and I'm a doctor, so this conversation doesn't bother me, but you're blushing. And as much as I enjoy that shy part of you, because it drives me crazy, and I want to fuck you on the table again, we have to be able discuss these things. If you can't talk to me, who can you talk to?" With a couple of scoots to the side, he brought his chair nearer to hers and kissed her. "I want to satisfy you, but I can't read your mind, so you have to tell me what you need. What do you want, George?"

"No one's ever asked me that question." And she'd never considered it. What was she supposed to do, when the greatest portion of her personality consisted of and revolved around other people's desires?

"That's a sin and a shame, babe." He picked up her fork and fed her a mix of egg and bacon. "You're the most generous, selfless person I've ever met, and yet I'd bet you never spare a second for yourself. Maybe that's why I'm here."

"Okay. I love it when you call me babe." In that instant, George tensed her thighs. "No one's ever called me babe, and I like it."

"Well, there's that." Grasping the underside of her seat, he yanked her closer and licked the curve of her jaw. "What else, *babe*?"

"My eggs." Raging passion surged, coupling with her impulses, as Rafe trailed his lips along the crest of her ear, and his breath quickened. Voicing her wants offered a new and exciting experience, and she struggled to control the emotions wreaking havoc within her, in concert with his cravings. "While I appreciate the breakfasts, and I'll eat whatever you fix, I prefer scrambled, with cheddar cheese, a couple of tablespoons of hot sauce, and a dash of seasoned salt."

"Duly noted and sounds delicious." As he brushed his nose to hers, he snatched a cinnamon roll and brought it to her mouth.

"Tell me more."

"I want you to know me." A confession danced on the tip of her tongue, yet she hesitated. "If it's all the same to you, I would have you know everything about me."

"I'm working on it." He massaged the back of her neck. "You could start by sharing your age. How old are you?"

"I can't believe you asked that." In mock affront, she elbowed him in the ribs and giggled. "Don't suppose it matters, but I'm twenty-six. Is that too old for you?"

"Are you kidding?" In a flirty manner, he toyed with the hair at her nape. "You're just right. And I'm thirty-two, by the way."

"Oh, but that's ancient." When he pinched her bottom, she yelped. "And I'd blow you into next Saturday, if you'd share the recipe for your coffee blend, because it's amazing."

"You're on." Laughing, Rafe tempted her with another sweet treat. "What about your favorite color?"

That was easy. "Yellow, inspired by the sunrise."

Patting his thighs, he arched a brow. "Flower?"

In response to his unmistakable invitation, George pushed from the table, stepped about his knees, turned to the side, and planted herself in his lap. "The red rose, because it symbolizes love."

"Bet I could've guessed that one." Untying her robe, he snorted. "You've got 'em all over your place."

"Maybe I'm just predictable." She gasped, as he inched his hand between her legs.

"Somehow, I doubt that." When he buried his face in her neck, she closed her eyes. "How soon do you need to leave? When do you have to open the tavern, at the latest?"

"Tony's already there." She moaned, as he touched her where she wanted it most. "He likes to get an early start on the cooking for the lunch rush."

"So you can spare an extra hour or two?" In little circles, he caressed a particularly sensitive spot. "Because I want to kiss you right there."

"*Oh.*" Blissful heat unfolded and spread, and she dropped back her head, as he drew her breast into his mouth. "I can, for the right incentive, and you're speaking my language."

All activity ceased, as he stood, carrying her with him. "Let's go upstairs."

"What for?" Of course, she knew what he wanted. "The table works for me."

"Not for me." Clutching her wrist, Rafe

raced down the hall. "I'm going to make love to you like I should have, last night."

CHAPTER FOUR

In the two weeks he'd been dating George, Rafe had yet to take her on a real date, and she hadn't complained. If he tried that crap with a big city girl, she'd have dumped his ass flat or demanded a truckload of flowers, an expensive dinner, and possibly jewelry, along with a lot of groveling. But his small town lady took it in stride when he canceled plans in the eleventh hour not once but four separate occasions.

True to character, when he couldn't make lunch, she brought him a burger and a salad. When he got stuck and worked late, she had a hot meal waiting on him. When he pulled a third shift, after Dr. Samuels got sick, she cooked breakfast, gave Rafe a mind-numbing blowjob, and tucked him between the covers.

Best of all, she warmed his bed every night, in what had become a cherished routine, so he resolved to make their Friday evening special, just for his sexy bartender.

In his pocket, his phone buzzed, and he checked the display.

George: Miss you.

Okay, he grinned like a lovesick idiot, as he typed a response.

Rafe: Been thinking about you all day.

George: Thank you for the flowers. They're beautiful.

Rafe: They're roses. You're beautiful, and you're welcome.

George: So excited about our date. Went shopping for something sexy…

Damn. She could arouse him in the middle of the busy ER.

Rafe: Lace?

George: Not telling. You'll have to wait and see.

Rafe: Have you any idea how hard it is to work with an enormous erection?

George: No. How hard is it?

Rafe: Very funny. Don't get dressed. Gonna jump your bones as soon as I get my hands on you.

George: Promises, promises.

Rafe: Want you naked when I get there.

George: When do you get off?

Rafe: Hopefully about five minutes after I arrive,

because we have a reservation.

George: I meant when do you leave the hospital?

Oh, he knew what she meant.

Rafe: Barring any unforeseen emergency, about 10 minutes.

George: I'm stripping.

And he was raring to go.

"Dr. Owen, if you're ready to release the gentleman in triage, you need to sign the chart, and I believe that's your last case." At the status board, Minnie erased a couple of names, updated the condition on two other patients, and listed assignments for the graveyard shift. "And did I ever tell you about my pretty, single granddaughter?"

"Sorry, Minnie." He palmed his phone. "But I'm taken."

"Really?" The head nurse sniffed. "Well that Mary-George is a lucky lady."

"Actually, I think I'm the lucky one." With a wink, he saluted and marched to an available terminal. In his brain, the sliver that remained functional and on task, he composed adequate instructions for follow-up care and recovery. Just as he entered the data, his phone vibrated.

George: I'm in your bed, and nothing comes between the sheets and me.

Rafe: Except me…I'm on my way.

His feet barely touched the ground as he ran to his car. After securing the seatbelt, he shifted into gear and charged out of the parking lot. With an eye out for a local cop or a county deputy, he sped down River Road and pulled into his driveway about four minutes later.

When Rafe walked into his bedroom, he found George nude, lying on her belly, and propped on her elbows. "There is a god."

Then he did exactly as he'd promised.

Approximately thirty minutes later, showered, shaved, and satisfied, he drove them into town, tapping his fingers on the wheel to the beat of the song playing on the satellite radio.

"This is a beautiful car." Studying the dashboard, she stretched in the seat. "I've never been in a Mercedes."

"Really?" He turned down the music. "Well, some might think I bought it to pad my ego, but the truth is it's comfortable, and that's important, given I travel all along the eastern seaboard. Plus, it's safe, which is critical to me."

"It rides like a dream." Twisting the climate control knob, she turned up the heat on her side.

"You ride like a dream. By the way, thanks

for that amazing quickie. I'd have been cursed with a wicked hard-on all night if you hadn't taken pity on me." He grabbed her hand and pressed his lips to the back of her knuckles. "You're blushing again. You do that whenever we talk about sex, and I adore you for it."

"I'm sorry." To his surprise, she bowed her head, as if in shame.

"Hey, I meant what I said. I love that reserved quality about you." At a stoplight, he leaned over and kissed her. "Don't go quiet on me, George. What's wrong? Have I done something to upset you?"

"I'm not as knowledgeable as you, in the bedroom, and I wonder if I'm experienced enough to maintain your interest." Picking at the hem of her sleeve, she frowned. "What if you get bored?"

"Are you kidding?" A quick scan of the parking lot offered numerous choices, and he pulled into a spot near the entrance of The Judges Chambers, a five-star restaurant occupying a grand old home, which Minnie swore would impress George. After exiting the car, he walked to the passenger side and opened the door for his lady. "Wait a second." Rafe drew her into his arms. "I took River Road at seventy-miles-per-hour to get home to you, just so I could fuck you six ways from Sunday, because I can't get enough of you, and you're worried I might get bored?"

"I don't know." As had become her habit, she avoided his stare when the discussion turned serious, so he cupped her chin and brought her gaze to his. What he spied in her blue eyes left him reeling.

"You really have no idea how much I want you." Of course, what he neglected to share was his attraction to the irresistible tavern owner confused him, too. Petite in stature, with generous curves in all the right places, she had nothing in common with his usual game, which tended toward the tall, slender, model-type. Those relationships possessed all the warmth and charm of a soggy piece of cardboard, whereas George seemed to inhabit every aspect of his life. "When I'm with you, I feel like the most important man in the world, such that when we're apart, I can't get you out of my head. When I'm not with you, I wonder where you are, if you're safe, if you're having a good day, and when I'll see you again. While we've fallen into a routine, of sorts, there's nothing routine about you or my attachment to you."

"I'm so glad to hear you say that." The

relief in her expression, and her shimmering smile, eased his concerns. "And you're not the problem. There's something I need to tell you, tonight, but I want to wait until we get back to your house."

"Okay, as long as we're all right." Twining his fingers in hers, he led her to the main entrance. "Until then, let's enjoy our dinner, some fine wine, and great conversation. And we might just skip the show at the Opera House, because I'm excited to find out what you're hiding under your skirt." To the host, Rafe said, "The name is Owen, and I have a reservation."

"Of course." The older gentleman, clothed in a tuxedo, collected a couple of menus. "This way, sir."

Filled with gently used antiques, including tables covered in heavily starched white linens, the distinguished dining room of The Judges Chambers featured burgundy velvet drapes, leather wall coverings, soft candlelight, and classical music performed by a string quartet positioned in a corner. In an alcove large enough to accommodate seating for two, Rafe held her chair. After unbuttoning his dinner jacket, he sat to her immediate left.

"Your server will be right with you." The host draped a napkin in George's lap. "Enjoy your evening."

"Uh-oh. I suppose I should have explained, and I hope you're not disappointed." She peered from side to side and leaned close. "I bought the dress for the occasion, and I'm not wearing any undies."

"Are you serious?" His mouth watered, when she blushed and nodded. And she worried he'd get bored. "You think I'm disappointed? Baby, you could bounce quarters off my dick right now."

"Well that's a lovely thought, and maybe we'll try it for an unconventional encore." He savored her throaty laughter and carefree spirit, as she flirted with him. "Should we order a bottle of chardonnay?"

"You must've read my mind, because that's my favorite." Once again, her uncanny ability to guess his choice amazed him. "Don't you think it's funny that our tastes are so similar? Maybe it's a sign."

"It's certainly something." Under the table, she clutched his hand, and she glowed. Then and there, he decided he'd do whatever it took to maintain that radiance, because in her joy he found purpose.

Despite graduating at the top of his class at med school, regardless of his luck with women, and notwithstanding his professional success, with George, he believed he could conquer mountains, swim the seas, and vanquish all enemies. Indeed, in her company, he was invincible, yet she remained a mystery to him, and he vowed to change that.

"You've never told me what you do for fun." As a tactician gathering evidence, he launched his plan to achieve his aim. "What are your hobbies?"

"That's easy." She averted her gaze. "I love to hike the woods behind the tavern, and I would give anything to share them with you, on a clear day."

"That's incredible, because I'm an avid hiker." A skeptic, he'd never believed in fairy tales, romance, and soul mates, but she may have swayed him in her favor, because she seemed made for him.

Little by little, inasmuch as a delicate rosebud spreads its petals and blossoms, his bartender shed her shyness, and the sassy goddess emerged. Recounting various stories from her past, George shared her personal history, marked by her reliable generosity.

"I got suspended in the fifth grade for fighting." She twirled a lock of her brown hair. "This horrible bully terrorized everyone at school, but I figured out he was afraid of anyone challenging him, so he intimidated them, first. One afternoon, after lunch, I confronted him and kicked his shins. He cried like a girl, and I got in trouble, but it was worth it, because he didn't bother us again."

"Ah, George, the great defender, always rushing to aid the less fortunate." When the waiter cleared their empty plates, Rafe sat back in his chair and studied his woman. "I'll bet you fought in pigtails and a frilly dress, too, because you're awfully at home in that little black number you're wearing."

"Don't forget the lace-trimmed ankle socks." In that instant, she shimmied her toes up his pants leg.

"I knew it." Spearing his fingers at her nape, he drew her close for a lengthy kiss. "God, you're beautiful, inside and out. Sure I can't talk you into forgoing *An Evening With Patsy Cline*?"

"This is our first date, sort of, and I want to revel in every minute of it." Yet, she skimmed her fingers beneath his napkin and caressed his erection. "Please. I promise, I'll take care of you, later, but I really want to spend time with you beyond the kitchen and your bedroom."

"That sounds fair." Cupping her cheek, he claimed another kiss. "And I'm not sure I can refuse you anything."

So for her sake, Rafe endured the small town production set in the past, at a performance by the legendary country singer, Patsy Cline. Although he enjoyed the collection of songs, the music had nary an impact, as he focused on his fascinating companion.

At his side, she perched on the edge of her seat and craned her neck, unabashed in her delight. During intermission, they made out behind a row of stalls that once held pay phones. Afterward, in his car, while they lingered at a stoplight, George bent and initiated a soul-stirring blowjob, and he pulled over before he hit a curb. When he finally turned right onto River Road, she zipped his pants, wiped her mouth, and refastened her seatbelt.

"I'm not done with you." Riding a crest of unquenchable lust, he inched his hand beneath her dress, found her sans panties, just as she claimed, and hot and slick between her thighs. "Fuck. You weren't kidding."

"Nope, but the reason is somewhat selfish." She snickered. "You've destroyed six pairs of my underwear. At this rate, I'll have none left in a week."

"And that's a problem?" He slipped a

finger inside her, and she moaned. "If you want, I'll get you some more—what the hell?"

A familiar SUV blocked his driveway, so he parked in George's, because she kept her truck in the garage. Even without glimpsing the New York license plate, he recognized the green Range Rover.

"Were you expecting visitors?" Grasping his wrist, she pushed free of him and tugged down the hem of her dress.

"No, but that wouldn't stop them." Pissed, he turned off the engine, got out of the car, and walked to the passenger side. "Come on, baby. I think you're about to meet my parents."

"Wait—what?" Shock evident in her expression, she halted. "Are you joking?"

"Unfortunately, no." He ushered her up the steps. "Promise you'll stay with me."

As they approached the porch, Rafe's father opened the door. "It's about time you got here."

"Nice to see you, too." In the living room, Rafe spotted his mother. "You didn't tell me you were driving up from Manhattan."

"We thought we'd surprise you, given we haven't spoken since the day you arrived in Haven Harbor, when you mentioned the spare key beneath the mat at the side entrance." His mom glanced at George. "Rafe, aren't you going to introduce us?"

Damn. He should've kept his mouth shut.

"Mom, Dad, this is my girlfriend, Mary-George McBride." He slipped an arm about George's waist, and she tensed. "Babe, this is Bill and Cynthia Owen."

"Hi." Stiffening her spine, George waved. "Well, it's getting late, and I should go." She retreated and almost tripped over the ottoman. "But it's no problem, because I live in the next house."

"How convenient." His father frowned.

"Wait, George." He glanced at his parents and cursed under his breath. "Don't go."

"It was lovely to meet you." Mother drew George from Rafe. "I look forward to becoming better acquainted some other time, but we have private business to discuss with our son. I'm sure you understand."

Typical. In the space of two minutes, his family insulted his lady and attempted to dictate his life, because he knew exactly what they intended, and he'd reject their proposal, as usual.

"Of course." George nodded once. "Goodnight."

"Hang on, babe." To his parents, Rafe said, "I'll be right back." Outside, he walked her to her porch. "I'm sorry, but they're a couple of real jerks, so don't take it personally."

"Don't say that." On tiptoes, she kissed him, and he pulled her into his arms. It dawned on him then that he'd found home in George's embrace. More important, he'd found acceptance, and he wasn't going to jeopardize that for anyone. "I'd give anything to have my parents here, and you never know what tomorrow will bring."

"You're right, but I know what's going to happen tonight, after I send them to bed." He patted her round ass. "Go inside, and don't undress, because that's my treat. Meet me at your kitchen door in ten minutes."

~

Sunday dinner at granny's house reigned supreme, as a longstanding family tradition, and any man interested in a future with George had to pass inspection. While some overprotective parents grilled prospective sons-in-law about occupations, finances, and children, granny was most concerned about some hotshot city fella taking George from Haven Harbor.

"You're awfully quiet. Did I tell you I got tomorrow off, so we can hike the woods behind the tavern?" Holding her hand, Rafe dropped a series of kisses across her knuckles, as he drove down Main Street. "Again, I apologize for yesterday. I shouldn't have brought my parents to the tavern for dinner, but I missed you. They were a royal pain in the butt, I hadn't seen you all day, you had to work a double, and I knew you wouldn't get home until late, so I thought it was a great idea."

What he neglected to mention was he needed validation—lots of it, and she didn't require any special powers to figure out why.

"I'll text Tony, and let him know I won't be in until Tuesday, because I'm going to spend time with my man. And it's okay about your parents." Actually, it wasn't okay, but what happened wasn't his fault. Although she tried to see the best in people, his mother and father tested George's patience with their ridiculous demands and general rudeness. No, her restaurant didn't serve *haute cuisine*, and yes she knew what that was, and she'd never won the James Beard Award, but her place served good, hot food at a reasonable price. And she hadn't worked a double. Dan Nutter, the librarian, called a coven meeting, and she couldn't explain that to Rafe, because she hadn't told him about her gift, so she lied, and she hated herself for it. "I'm just glad you came over last night, because I'm not sure I can sleep without you. Don't know what I'm going to do after you leave Haven Harbor."

"After the way they treated you, I couldn't stay away, babe. Plus, they never drag out of bed before nine, so there was no reason I couldn't fix our breakfast, as usual." With his thumb, he drew circles on her palm and didn't take the bait. And he said nothing about the way his parents treated their own son, which she found unutterably sad, because it suggested their behavior was common practice. While he pretended to pay no attention to their criticism, his energy conveyed the opposite. No wonder he wanted to escape them. "I'm so sorry, but you bore the brunt of their anger, when you did nothing wrong."

"I don't understand." Shifting in her seat, it bothered her that he ignored her comment, in regard to his impending departure. What was she going to do without him? "Why are they angry?"

"Because my father wants me to take a job in his hospital, and I told him I've decided to accept the position of Chief of ER Medicine at Haven Harbor Regional, on a permanent basis." Now that was a revelation. At a red light, he met her stare. "Josiah Adams made the official offer last week, after the board approved it, and I'm taking it." In play, he nibbled the tip of her finger, as he yearned for approval. "Everything I could ever want is right here, in Haven Harbor."

"So you're not going away?" Relieved, she could have cried, and tears welled, especially when his inner dialogue confirmed his words, and then her emotions interfered, acting as a barrier to her gift. "I won't have to figure out how to sleep without you or recall how to make my own breakfast, because you've spoiled me?"

"Hey, no water works, babe. You're stuck with me, unless you decide otherwise, because I couldn't leave you if I tried, and I'm glad to know I'm good for something." Rafe winked, as he turned onto Raven Road. "Does that put you at ease?"

"Yes, but what about your parents?" Bill and Cynthia broadcast some serious aggression, and George didn't know what to make of them. "They don't like me, and it's the fourth house on the left."

"It's not about you, personally." He quirked his brows. "The one with the plastic pink flamingos in the yard? What are there, six or seven?"

"Granny's always dreamed of living in

Florida, and that's as close as she got. In fact, she proudly owns the entire collection of *Miami Vice* on DVD, which she watches every Saturday night." When he pulled into the driveway and shifted into park, she released her seatbelt and faced him. "And if it's not me, then what's the problem? What do your parents want?"

"It's Haven Harbor." Leaning forward, he cupped her chin. "They hate anything that doesn't involve my residing and working in New York, but it's not their choice. I've never planned to remain in Manhattan."

And he wanted to move in with George, which his energy all but screamed.

Stunned by his news, and the level of commitment he contemplated with her, she met him halfway and pressed her lips to his. "Let's go inside, and tonight, when we get home, I want to curl up on the couch with you and talk about the rental, the holidays, and where we go from here."

"You read my mind, beautiful." Of course, she had. As always, he exited and then opened her door, like a perfect gentleman. "And I bet you know what else I want, tonight." There was the not-so-perfect gentleman...

"Oh, I require no special abilities to figure

that out, because you're pretty reliable in that department." Smiling, she took his hand in hers, as they climbed the porch steps. If only he received the secret of her true powers with the same spirit, and she'd find out soon enough. For good or ill, she had to tell him the truth, before he discovered it on his own. "So I'll be sure not to eat too much, in preparation for all that bouncing."

"You know it, baby." Waggling his brows, he reached behind and pinched her ass. "And I bought some lube."

George burst into laughter.

"What's all that racket out there?" Looming in the entry, with arms folded, granny lifted her chin. That meant trouble of the mischievous kind. "You're five minutes late, and the food's getting cold."

"Sorry." George kissed her grandma on the cheek. "We went for a walk in the park and lost track of time." She peered over her shoulder. "I believe you two already know each other."

"Wait a minute." Halting, confusion investing his countenance, Rafe narrowed his stare. "You never told me Minnie Terwilliger was your grandmother."

"No, she didn't." Sporting the same haughty demeanor with which she supervised the ER nurses, granny snorted, and George gritted her teeth. "And if you'd taken my offer to meet my pretty young granddaughter, you wouldn't have survived long enough to be invited to dinner, because I knew you were dating Mary-George. Now get in here and wash your hands, because I'm ready to eat."

"Yes, ma'am." After cleaning his shoes on the mat, he crossed the threshold, and his hunger exploded in George's senses. "Something smells delicious."

"Granny makes the most incredible steak and dumplings." George showed him to the kitchen sink and flipped on the faucet. "And there are those who'd trade their firstborn for her cucumber salad recipe."

"Don't forget my award-winning dessert." With a twinkle in her eye, Minnie tossed a towel on the counter. "My Perilously Perverted Peach Cobbler Plague has won first place in the SFCCC the last three years, in a row."

"I beg your pardon?" Glancing at George, and silently pleading for salvation, Rafe scratched his temple and blinked. "What is the SFCCC?"

"What is the *SFCCC*?" Mouth agape, and with an owlish gaze, Minnie rested fists on hips, and George winced. "Am I dealing with a heathen? Why, everyone knows the Spooktacular Fang-tastic Cast-iron Cauldron Cook-off is the premiere event of the Haven County Fair, and I aim to claim my fourth blue ribbon next weekend, just you wait and see." Then she shooed him. "Now go grab a seat, because I'm so hungry I could eat my toenails."

"Grandma Minnie, stop it." George wagged a finger. "We talked about this, and you promised you'd be on your best behavior. You're trying to scare Rafe, in light of Russell Lee's absence, and that's not nice." She pulled out the long bench of the antique dining table and drew her man to the spot beside her. "You might want to be nice to Rafe, as I have it on good authority that he's about to be your new boss, on a permanent basis."

"You took the chief's position. I suppose I shouldn't be surprised, since I gave you my seal of approval." With a cackle, Minnie slapped a thigh. "About time that old coot Josiah retired." Then she wrinkled her nose. "Well there might be hope for you, yet, doc. Knew there had to be more to you than a pretty face."

"*Granny.*" Mortified, George peered at Rafe. Thankfully, all she sensed in him was a strong desire for food. "Does she talk like this at the hospital?"

"Worse." Rafe rolled his eyes. "And although I'm told I'm in charge of the ER, I have yet to supervise much if anything, because Nurse Terwilliger cracks the whip and runs the show. But everyone loves her, and I still can't figure out why."

"Just wait till I take a vacation, and you have to make do without me." Grandma dished healthy portions. "You'll be singing another tune."

"Maybe, 'Happy Days are Here Again?'" He grinned, and George held her breath. "Or, 'Ding Dong! The Witch Is Dead.'"

Slowly, Minnie smiled. "You're learning, doc."

In concert, they laughed.

Over dinner, the conversation ranged from such fascinating topics as proper suture techniques, bedsores, and gangrene, and George took it in stride, given Rafe and Minnie got along as two old friends. After cleaning his plate, he asked for seconds, and George could have kissed him, because that was the way to melt granny's heart.

"You did some serious damage, doc." Granny stacked the dishes, while George collected the silver. "Now let me fetch the grand finale, so good it'll slap you."

When Minnie entered the kitchen, George wrapped her arms about Rafe's shoulders and kissed him hard. "You're wonderful."

He studied her lips and then met her stare. "Just wait till I get you home."

"All right, prepare to be amazed." Granny set the Plague on the table. "Knock of the smooching and salute my magnificence."

"Wow." Rafe opened and then closed his mouth. "That looks like a heart attack in a bowl."

"Don't you disparage my signature fare, or I'll have to hurt you." In small dishes, Minnie scooped her killer confection and topped each serving with a massive dollop of whipped cream. Just as she sat, the phone rang. "Now who could that be on a Sunday evening? You two dig in, while I see who's on the clap trap."

Alone with her hot doc, George spooned the whipped cream and bit her bottom lip. "We could have fun with this."

"Oh, yea?" Rafe leaned near. "I'm more interested in your sweet cream." When she squealed, he gave her a quick peck. "You're blushing, and that drives me crazy. Wonder what Minnie would do if I bent you over the table and fucked you right here?"

"How about in the car, on the way home?"

Shielded by the linens, she squeezed his thigh. "We haven't christened the backseat, and since we both took off work tomorrow, for our hike in the woods, we can stay out late and relax in the morning."

"Mary-George, that was Melinda Connelly." Clutching a hand to her belly, granny, pale and overly emotional, rushed into the dining room. "Bo Stanton had a stroke, and she wants you to come to the hospital."

CHAPTER FIVE

Despite his high-dollar education, and the wealth of medical knowledge he possessed, there were moments in Rafe's life when he had no clear understanding of or explanation for the mysteries of the human body. In usual circumstances, time passed, and like the seasons that marked the world in transit, the vigor of youth waned, and people grew old. Such was the way of nature. But other cases puzzled him. One minute, a patient was fine. The next, the unfortunate soul breathed his last, regardless of modern medicine and technology. Somewhere in the middle, locked in an unresponsive body and incapable of speech, rested the once-cantankerous and animated Bo Stanton in Trauma One.

"According to Dr. Samuels, Bo was found in the park, face down on the ground." Rafe wrapped an arm about George's waist, to offer comfort and support. "No one knows how long he languished in that sorry state until a passing police officer, on routine patrol, found Bo. Given the delay in treatment, which can make all the difference in these instances, we have no way of knowing whether or not he'll survive, but he's suffered a massive stroke."

"He walks that path, every day, between the tavern and his house." Shaking her head, George wiped a stray tear from her cheek and pulled her phone from her purse. "Let me call Tony and ask if Bo made it for brunch."

"Babe, it doesn't matter whether or not Bo ate." Without doubt, he could almost read her thoughts and her line of reasoning, as she emitted a soft sob. "You couldn't have prevented it. These things happen, and we don't know why. What do you say we go home, I make some coffee, I build a fire in the hearth, we put in an old movie, we curl up on the couch, and we just relax?"

"I need to find Melinda, and we can't leave until we know something." Facing him, she snuggled closer. "What sort of treatment does Dr. Samuels recommend?"

"Well, that's where the situation gets complicated." Resting his chin atop her head, he tightened his hold. "Bo didn't have a DNR on file."

"What's that?" She sniffed.

"It's an order not to resuscitate, in the event he stops breathing or his heart stops beating." He rubbed her back. "Without a DNR, we have to code him. We have to take extra measures to revive him, which prolongs the situation, and there's nothing we can do about it."

"That sounds horrible. Just like my dad." Given her generous spirit, he'd bet she planned to stay until the bitter end. "What if Bo doesn't want that?"

"That's why I called Minnie." A young woman, who appeared similar in age to George, lingered near a cluster of snack machines. "I told Tom to take the kids home, so I can handle this, but I can't do it alone. Can you tell me what Pops wants, George?"

"Oh, Melinda, dear friend, of course I will." George wrenched from his grasp and flung herself at the Melinda, while Rafe tried to figure out the cryptic question and George's even more baffling reply. "Please, I'd like you to meet Dr. Rafe Owen. He's the new Chief of ER Medicine and my boyfriend." She peered at him. "Rafe, this is Melinda Connelly, Bo's daughter. We went to high school, together."

"It's nice to make your acquaintance, although I'm so very sorry about the circumstances." As would a gentleman, he shook Melinda's hand. "But I'm a little confused. How can George tell you what Bo wants, when he's unconscious?"

"By using her gift." Melinda didn't so much as blink, but she could have knocked him over with a feather. "If you're dating her, then you know George can read his thoughts and help me decide what to do, because I hold my father's medical power of attorney. Dr. Samuel's says it's up to me, but I don't want to take action, until I know what dad wants me to do."

"It's going to be okay, because I'll help you." His ears rang, as George hugged Melinda. "As long as he's alive, I can hear him. Take me to Bo."

"Wait—what the hell's going on here?" Stunned, he grabbed George by the wrist. "You can't be serious. This isn't a game. This isn't some bar trick where you guess a customer's favorite drink. You're talking about a man's life."

"Rafe, I'm sorry, and I hope you can

forgive me, but I have to go with Melinda, because Bo needs me." George pulled free and frowned. "I should have told you everything before now, and I meant to, but things kept getting in the way, and I was afraid. When we go home, I promise, I will withhold nothing. I will tell you everything."

"Everything about what?" He shuffled his feet. "You can't honestly believe you possess some wacko power to speak to an unconscious patient. By definition, he can't converse with you. He's totally incapacitated."

"Please, George." Melinda retreated a step. "We have to hurry."

"It's not some 'wacko power,' as you put it." George drew Melinda into a protective embrace. "Have you never had a hunch? Have you never trusted your gut, when examining a patient? Have you never experienced intuition and run with it?"

"But this isn't about a hunch, a gut instinct, or intuition." George whirled about, and he followed in their wake, as they marched past intake and through the double-door entry of the ER.

Dumbfounded by her staunch assertion that she could somehow communicate with Bo, and too engrossed to abandon her, Rafe kept a position in the rear, while George walked into the trauma unit. At bedside, she took Bo's hand in hers, as the machines played an eerie audial symphony of beeps and hisses.

"Hello, Bo." George gazed on him and smiled. "It's George, and I'm here to listen to you, my dear friend."

Then she closed her eyes and bowed her head.

Seconds ticked past on the wall clock, and the tension grew. For him, it was like witnessing a train wreck, in slow motion, and there was nothing he could do to avert disaster. Angry, he clenched and unclenched his fists, as George went about her business, or whatever she called it. When she came alert, he pushed from the wall and folded his arms.

"Bo wants to be with Mabel." George flicked her fingers, and Melinda neared. "He wants you to let go, but he wants you to be happy with his choice. You have to be strong, because he needs your permission to rest, or else he'll continue to fight the inevitable outcome." George withdrew. "Talk to him, Melinda. He can hear you, and you must release him. I can't free him. It has to come from you."

"Oh, Daddy, I love you." The daughter bowed her head and wept, and Rafe struggled to contain his fury. "You're not alone, because I'm with you. Whenever you're ready, just fly, Daddy. Fly."

As Melinda recalled treasured moments, all the while ensuring Bo that she'd be fine, because she had her husband and kids, Rafe glared at George. When he could take no more, he hauled her from the room, dragged her down the corridor, and pulled her into his office, whereupon he slammed shut the door.

"What the hell was that?" With fists on hips, he shifted his weight. "What do you think you're doing? You have no right to meddle in Bo's medical decisions—I don't give a damn what you believe you know about him. You're not a doctor, you have no training, you're not a blood relative, and you have no legal authority in the matter."

"I have a duty, to Melinda and myself, and that trumps all else." To his utter amazement, she had the audacity to stand her ground, absent the slightest trace of contrition. Squaring her shoulders, she lowered her chin. "While I owe you an explanation, and you deserve one, this is neither the time nor the place to have this discussion. Bo's dying, and I need to support my friend."

"He's dying because you condemned him to a certain fate, without any real knowledge of his condition." Raking his fingers through his hair, he paced behind his desk. "And you may have broken the law. I have half a mind to notify the police."

"Go ahead." With a cavalier attitude, she shrugged. "There are those who know of my abilities, and they would do nothing, because I didn't harm Bo. You said it, yourself, he's had a massive, debilitating stroke. For all your anger, which pours from you, did you ever actually stop and listen to what he's telling you? Put on your doctor's coat, reflect on everything Dr. Samuels detailed, and ask yourself what you would recommend, were Bo your patient."

"So you know what's best, because you claim to speak for him, based on some imaginary skill, which I don't buy for a minute." He halted and pinned her with his stare. "If you're so smart and powerful, why aren't you betting on sports games, levitating the Brooklyn Bridge, and touring the country, while conversing with spirits?" Rafe snorted. "You'd make a fortune, because you're pretty fucking convincing, George the Magnificent."

"Don't you dare insult me with such ridiculous ideas, because it's downright offensive. A witch, a term created by those with no concept of what I am, is nothing more than an ordinary person with an extraordinary capability. We're just like everyone else." Unmistakable ire invested her expression, as she bared her teeth, in an impressive display of temper. In fact, it was the most emotion she'd exhibited, outside the bedroom, since he'd known her, so he must've struck a nerve. "You're upset, so I'll overlook your ignorance and tolerate your slight. Right now, I'm going back to Melinda, because she's my priority, and if you don't understand that, then you're not the man I thought you were. Tomorrow, we'll sit down, I'll do my best to shed some light on my past, and we can decide whether or not we still have a future."

Without so much as a backward glance, she stomped from his office.

~

A clear blue sky welcomed the sun, as it rose on the horizon, marking a brand new day. As she laced her hiking boots, George mulled the past ten hours, wondered how everything had gone so horribly wrong, and yawned. After a long night at the hospital, she returned home to find Rafe's house dark, so she slept at her place, but she hardly rested, because she missed him at her side.

Standing, she peered out the window. Light shone from his kitchen, so she grabbed her zippered sweatshirt and her backpack, pushed on the screen door, yanked the oak panel shut behind her, locked the bolt, and raced across the two driveways.

When she twisted the knob of the secondary entrance of the rental, it didn't budge, so she knocked. Clinging to hope, to some small measure of compassion, she prayed he'd just forgot about the lock, because she usually stayed with him. As soon as he opened the door, she realized she was in trouble.

"No coffee and cinnamon rolls? Where's my chef?" The half-attempt at humor failed, as he remained stoic. The machine sat empty, as did the stovetop and the oven. "Do you want some help cooking?"

"How's Bo?" His acerbic tone sliced right through her, as did the contempt in his energy, which she failed to deflect.

"Gone." She noted the bowl of cold cereal on the table, and her heart sank. "He passed peacefully, just after three this morning, surrounded by Melinda, her husband Tom, and the grandkids."

"So, I guess that's it." Not once did he

spare her a glance, as he returned to his seat and picked up his spoon. "Why are you here?"

Palpable anger assailed her senses, but she refused to run and hide. Instead, she summoned courage. "Before I left you—"

"You mean before you walked out on me." Compressing his lips in a thin line, he pointed for emphasis. "Don't try to sugarcoat your actions."

"What did you expect me to do?" No polite pleasantries softened his fury, and she splayed her hands. "I didn't have time to school you on the basics of magick, with a –k, and my gift."

"Really?" With palms pressed to his thighs, and his inner dialogue running amok, such that she couldn't quite read him, Rafe inclined his head and narrowed his stare. "That's your story? That's the best you can do? You possess some sort of otherworldly ability, with no evidence to support you, and that makes everything okay?"

"No, it doesn't." Based on his unspoken sentiment, George feared it would never be okay. Still, she resolved to try and salvage something of their relationship. "But I can prove what I say is true."

"Proof is an interesting concept."

Everything within him declared his cynicism. "How?"

Desperate, she leaped at the chance. "Center your thoughts."

"And you're going to tell me what I'm thinking." It was a statement, not a question. Unmistakably skeptical, he smirked. "Okay. I'll play along."

Shaking, her confidence in tatters, she licked her lips and sifted through his aggression. With her heart hammering in her chest, and her pulse pounding in her ears, she struggled to focus. Grasping at metaphorical straws, she closed her eyes and reached for his thoughts. Awareness coalesced and dispersed, ebbed and flowed, as a gentle low tide, and every time she neared her goal, the perception shattered, scattering like so many autumn leaves floating in the breeze.

"I can't seem to concentrate." She swallowed hard, as he assailed her with a healthy dose of disbelief. "Maybe because I'm upset, and I care about you. I don't want to lose you, Rafe."

"How convenient." Never had he looked at her with such disdain, and she clenched her gut. "And you should've considered that last night."

Suddenly, a single coherent impression

dawned, and it killed her. "You want me to leave."

"Given the circumstances, that could be a lucky guess." To add insult to injury, he checked his wristwatch. "Anything else? I have to get to work."

"But you took today off, so we could go hiking." Defeated, she slumped her shoulders. "Is this the end? You refuse to hear me, and that's it?"

"I swapped shifts with another doctor, because I have nothing else to do, and what more do you have to say?" In that instant, he shut her out, as if slamming a door in her face. "To be honest, I can't figure out if you're delusional or just plain crazy as a loon, but I don't plan to stick around for the answer. I've changed my mind about the ER job, and I'm leaving at the end of the month."

"I think I knew that." Part of her died in that moment. "Can I tell you a story, if I start from the beginning?" If their relationship was over, George had no problem baring everything.

"Make it quick." What she would give to block her gift, to repel the scalding heat of his disgust. "I go on shift in an hour."

"All right." After pulling out a chair, she dropped her backpack and sat. "I was eight when I realized I wasn't like other kids. It began as a series of sensations, like a shiver, but I experienced what can only be described as silent communication, for lack of a better expression."

"Did you talk back to it?" Now he made fun of her, because he wanted to hurt her, but she refused to take the bait.

"At first, I couldn't unravel the messages." She shrugged. "I was young, and some of the emotions were beyond my level of comprehension. And I didn't know how to control my power, so it overwhelmed and frightened me. I tried to ignore it, but it impacted my schoolwork, I withdrew from my friends, and I rebelled. One day, my father took me from class, we hiked the woods behind the tavern, and he explained the situation in simple concepts that I could grasp."

"Your father?" Rafe furrowed his brow. "Why not your mother? Women are witches, right?"

"Because I inherited the insight from his side of the family." She believed his question, although a little on the nasty side, a positive sign. "While modern professionals refer to my ability as claircognizance, in elementary language, it means I can read people. I can decipher their energy; only mine is a little more fine-tuned than that, because I know what people want. I read their hopes, their desires, and their needs. I hear what they want. Early in my practice, I had trouble sharpening my focus, as the intuition came to me in a tidal wave of intention and emotion, and I couldn't manage it. At times, it made me physically ill, yet I couldn't escape it. But my father worked with me, showed me how to relax, taught me to hone my craft, to focus and not just accept but to welcome the blessing of my birth. And as I said last night, you've probably experienced the same thing; only you know it as a hunch or a gut instinct, because most doctors are intuitive people. But it's the same thing."

"That's how you guessed my drinks correctly, when I came into the tavern that night?" At last, she'd caught Rafe's attention, as he manifested curiosity. Then he averted his gaze. "And the food—you knew exactly what I'd planned to order."

"Yes." With a steely grip on her faith in him, George nodded. "From the minute you walked into the tavern and lusted over my ass, I've known everything you wanted."

"The eggs." She could almost detect the squeaky rasp of the gears grinding in his brain, as he worked it through. "When I asked how you preferred them, you said sunny side up, which is my favorite. Later, you explained that you like them scrambled." Counting on his fingers, he mumbled to himself, and hope glimmered, as his anger receded. "Then there was the wine. You picked a chardonnay, when we dined at The Judges Chambers."

"Because it was your preference." Yes, he inundated her with a slew of emotions, and she reached across the table, but he refused to take her hand. "I only wanted to make you happy."

"How? By lying to me?" In a rush, he pushed from his chair, paced, paused by the counter, and pounded the granite top, and she jumped when she realized she'd misread him. "By pretending to be something you're not? You claim to enjoy hiking, but did you say that because you know it's my hobby? Do I even know you, or was it a façade to lure me into a relationship?"

"Of course, you know me, probably better than anyone." From his perspective, she appeared a chameleon, and he wanted nothing to do with her. That desire she read, loud and clear. "And I told you, my father used to take me hiking. It became our ritual, until his death."

"How can I believe you?" He huffed a breath. "How do I know you didn't just make up that story to fool me? How can I ever trust you, again?"

"Because you know me." To her infinite regret, he slipped from her grasp, in more ways than one. "But you want no part of me." In fact, his thoughts had traveled full circle, to where they started. "When my parents were hit on ninety-five, my mother died at the scene, but my father lingered in a coma for four months. *For four months.*" As tears streamed her cheeks, she gathered her backpack and stood. "The doctors tried everything, but he suffered, and I was powerless to stop it. All the while, he begged me to set him free, in his thoughts, every minute of every hour of every day of every week, but I could do nothing, because he never made any plans. So I put my life on hold and maintained a constant vigil, as he died a little more with each sunset, and part of me was lost with him, when he finally passed. I'm sorry about Bo, but if I had it to do over again, I wouldn't change a thing. I couldn't live with myself if I denied Melinda's request, ignored Bo's wishes, and let what happened with my father occur again, when I could prevent it."

Painful silence filled the kitchen, and then and there she vowed to sell both houses after Rafe departed, as the memories of what transpired there would destroy her. In the quiet, she sought a connection with him, one last time. When she detected his energy, she flinched.

"I need to get to work." In that instant, she recalled that first morning they had breakfast together and his similar statement coupled with a strong desire for her company. Then, Rafe didn't want to let go. Now, he wanted George gone.

As was her way, she would give him what he wanted.

"I'm sorry I intruded on your breakfast. It won't happen again, and my leasing agent will complete the rental agreement when you vacate the property." She walked to the door, rested her palm to the cool metal knob and delayed, ever so slightly. He could stop her. With a single word, he could have her. "But I don't regret what I did, because I could never lie to someone who wants the truth. This is who I am, and I couldn't change if I tried. However, if I had a choice, I wouldn't trade my gift for anything, because I help people. I know what they want, and I give it to them, or I find a way to get it to them. No matter what you think, that can't be bad."

CHAPTER SIX

The wind thrummed and howled, as it rolled in from the ocean, heralding the rapid approach of a surprise storm. Sitting at a small picnic table set up for visitors, near the ER, with a great view of the sea, Rafe shivered and checked his remaining break time. It was a good thing he'd cancelled the planned hike in the woods with George. Just as fast, he reminded himself they were no longer a couple.

Yet he couldn't stop thinking about her.

In his mind, he replayed their conversation that morning, and the events that preceded Bo's death. No matter how hard he tried to condemn the beautiful bartender, he couldn't deny one simple, nagging fact.

George had a good heart.

If she indeed possessed some preternatural power, and he still wasn't entirely convinced, a sincere desire to help people underscored her every action, when she could have used such ability to her advantage. Instead, she cooked casseroles for the senior citizens center potluck lunch. Given his occupation, he had to acknowledge the possibility she was telling the truth, because science couldn't explain everything in the universe.

A clap of thunder roared, and he flinched. An eerie sensation traipsed his spine, and he rubbed the back of his neck. After fishing his phone from his pocket, he scrolled to her contact and texted a brief message.

Rafe: You okay?

Nothing.

"What's up, doc?" Carrying a lunch bag and a soda, Minnie cackled. "Got a hot date with Mary-George?"

"No." Still no response, and he frowned. "Excuse me a second, Minnie."

Walking to the ridge-line, he dialed George's number. When she didn't answer, he composed himself and waited for the beep. "George, it's me." The words that had seemed so difficult to utter that morning now flowed freely. "I'm sorry. I'm an ass, and I was wrong about everything. Please, call me back, even if it's just to tell me to go to hell. I need to know you're all right."

Amid the ominous black clouds building to the east, a bolt of lightning zigzagged across the sky, and he strolled to the verge.

"Looks like the weather-guessers got it wrong again." Shaking her head, Minnie humphed. "The ache in my bad hip forecasts rain better than those yahoos in Boston, especially since Estelle's radar is down."

"Hey, Minnie, have you spoken to George today?" To his disappointment, his cell remained silent. "I tried to reach her, but she's not picking up, and I'm worried."

"Well, let me see." The head nurse produced an antiquated flip phone with extra large buttons. Wrinkling her nose, she made a few selections and held the device to her ear. With a huff, she narrowed her stare. "Mary-George, this is your grandma. You know I don't much appreciate conversing with these infernal contraptions, so you give me a ring." As she studied her phone, Minnie scratched her chin. "It ain't like Mary-George to ignore me, but I know she was real upset over Bo. Maybe she needs some time to herself."

"Do you think she'd have gone hiking without me?" When George visited him that morning, she wore boots. "I swapped schedules at the last minute, and I know she was excited about exploring the woods behind the tavern, with me."

Slowly, with an expression of astonishment, Minnie met his gaze, and tears welled in her eyes. "She was going to take you hiking in those woods?"

"Yea." He sat beside the nurse. "What's wrong? You're white as a sheet."

"Oh, my lord." Minnie slapped her thigh and chuckled. "I knew Mary-George was crazy about you, but I didn't realize it was that serious."

"I don't understand." A strange tightening in his chest had him struggling for breath. "What's so important about hiking?"

"You know about her parents." When he nodded, Minnie sighed, drew a tissue from her pocket, and blew her nose with an ear-piercing trumpet blast. "You ever tell anyone you saw me cry, and I'll assign all the hemorrhoid cases to you, leave your name with the night nurse, as the on-call doc, and instruct her to pester you every fifteen minutes."

"Your secret is safe with me." He patted her hand.

"Well, after her daddy passed, Mary George spent months wandering in those woods. I was so afraid for her, and I knew she was hurting, but she wouldn't share it with me." Minnie sniffed and cast a hint of a smile. "That girl devotes herself to the happiness of those around her, and she'd give you the shirt off her back, but I'll be damned if she'll do anything for herself. If she finally decided to let someone in, I'm glad it was you."

And Rafe threw that golden opportunity in George's face.

But all was not lost, and he vowed he'd get her back. The alarm on his timer signaled the end of his break, and he cursed. "Do me a favor. Keep trying to reach her. I can't explain why, but I have a bad feeling."

"Will do, doc." Minnie snapped her fingers. "In fact, I'll call Tony. I'll bet she's at the tavern."

"You're probably right, and I don't know why I didn't think of that." Yet the nagging sense of foreboding loomed, and he rolled his shoulders. "Let me know when you find her, and ask her to text me."

With that, he returned to the ER, but before he took his next patient, he sent another message.

Rafe: Please, forgive me. I need you. I want you, and you always give people what they want.

And so he continued his shift, diagnosing a

nasty bout of the flu, identifying a severe case of 'fluff my pillow' syndrome, suturing a gash to a brow, and immobilizing a sprained wrist. When he realized he could no longer function, because he still hadn't heard from his bartender, he checked his phone for the hundredth time. He couldn't focus, because everything in him centered on George. It occurred to him then, in the quiet of his mind, that she was right in so many ways, and her ability wasn't that far-fetched.

As a physician, he relied heavily on instinct, or what many physicians referred to as clinical intuition, as opposed to results-driven methodology based on lab test outcomes. When he assessed patients, he catalogued a list of their complaints and then consulted his gut reaction—his hunch, to prescribe treatment.

In that instant, his gut told him George was in trouble.

At the nurses station, he searched for Minnie. "Has anyone seen Nurse Terwilliger?"

"She stepped outside to take a personal call." A pharmacy tech collected prescriptions from a basket. "I'm sure she'll be right back."

A few strides brought him to intake, and he pushed through the double doors. When Minnie spotted him, she waved frantically.

"About an hour ago, Tony found George's truck parked in the lot behind the tavern, but she's not at work, so he called the sheriff." Closing her eyes, Minnie pressed a clenched fist to her mouth. "The deputies, Tony, and several of the tavern employees launched a search, but it's storming nine kinds of hell, and I just know she's in those woods, all alone."

"I need to get out there." He ripped his stethoscope from his neck and unbuttoned his white coat but stopped. "Shit. I need to find someone to cover for me."

"I already called Josiah, and he's on his way." Furrowing her brow, Minnie peered at the driving rain beyond the windows of the waiting room. "Bring her home safe, doc."

"I will." Determined to find George, so he could prostrate himself at her feet and beg forgiveness, he charged outside as he dug his hand into his pants pocket. "Fuck. My keys are on my desk."

With a sharp about face, he ran into the ER, retraced his steps, sprinted into his office, and snatched his keys from the blotter. At intake, Dr. Adams closed his umbrella, daubed his forehead with a paper towel, and shrugged from his soaked raincoat.

"Dr. Adams." Rafe shook Josiah's

outstretched hand. "Aren't you supposed to be on vacation?"

"My idea of a vacation is sleeping late, having lunch with my son, taking my grandkids to school, and beating Bart Jandrucko at dominoes at the senior citizens center, every afternoon." The senior physician smiled. "Although, if I take much more of his retirement money, Hazel might leave him, and what would Lometa and I do on bridge night?" Then he sobered. "Any word on Mary-George?"

Behind the nurses station, the radio buzzed, and a voice cut through the static. "Haven Harbor ER, this is Rescue One."

A chill of dread shook Rafe to his core.

"I'll get that." Josiah rushed to the mic and depressed the button. "Go ahead, Rescue One."

"En route to your location, one time. Twenty-six year old white female fell approximately fifteen feet into a ravine. Patient was unconscious on arrival. Patient is now conscious, semi alert, and somewhat disoriented. Possible fracture of left ankle. BP one-forty over eighty. Pulse seventy-six. Respirations sixteen. ETA ten minutes."

"Haven Harbor, clear." Dr. Adams glanced at Rafe. "I know emotions are high, but let's not jump to conclusions, folks."

Fear stretched taut Minnie's expression, and she stared at Rafe, as her lips trembled. "You don't think that's—" In her pocket, her phone rang, and she flipped open the device. "Hello? Yes?" Almost instantly, tears formed, she pinned him with her horror, and he knew it was George. "Thank you, for letting me know. We're waiting for her."

From every angle, the walls seemed to collapse on him, and beneath his feet the floor pitched and rolled. Leaning against the counter for support, he clenched his teeth, and his knees buckled.

There were moments in Rafe's life when he opted for a path of least resistance, so often driven by anger, which led to nothing but disappointment and regret. In a sliver of time marked by frustration and a desire for revenge, he yielded to his emotions and acted in haste, always with disastrous consequences. It was only afterward, when the emotional fog cleared, that he discovered he could have spared himself the ensuing anguish had he taken just a few minutes to listen, to reflect, and to reason. Forever, he would torture himself with the belief that had he chosen otherwise, George would be all right.

As the staff scattered in various directions,

preparing to receive her, he stood silent, while something inside him fractured. It began as a small fissure, which snaked and coiled through him, tearing at his gut, eating at his conscience, and shredding his confidence. When the blare of the siren neared, followed by silence, signaling the ambulance's arrival, he turned and ran straight into Josiah.

"Where do you think you're going?" Dr. Adams arched a brow. "You cannot treat your girlfriend, Dr. Owen, and you know that."

"Don't throw me out, because I can't leave her." Desperate, Rafe splayed his palms. "I'll stay in the hall, out of your way, but I'm not going to sit in the waiting room, like a civilian."

"If you interfere, in any way, I'll call security." Josiah turned to Minnie. "That goes for you, too, Nurse Terwilliger."

A flurry of activity surrounded George, as the paramedics rolled her into the ER and the Trauma Unit. Mobilized by a C-collar, and with blood oozing from her forehead, she moaned. For a few seconds, her lashes fluttered, and then she opened her eyes. As soon as she noted his presence, recognition dawned, and she recoiled. That damn near broke him.

For the next couple of hours, he paced, and Minnie maintained her vigil at the opening to the privacy curtain. If only he could talk to George. If only he could tell her how sorry he was for the way he behaved. Then it hit him. He could speak to her on her level, in her unique language.

What was it she asked of him that morning?

Center your thoughts.

Closing his eyes, Rafe unlocked the door to his heart, freed his mind, and took a leap of faith.

He believed she could hear him.

He believed she would understand him.

He believed she would forgive him.

He believed.

"Dr. Owen, Mary-George is asking for you." When Rafe opened his eyes, Dr. Adams smiled. "She has fractures to the left fibula, tibia, and talus, which may require surgery, bruised ribs, multiple contusions, and a mild closed head injury. All in all, she's in good shape, but I'd like to keep her for a couple of days, and if her recovery goes well, you may take her home, Wednesday."

"Thank you, sir." Rafe exhaled in relief. To Minnie, he said, "Can I have a minute with George, alone?"

"Of course." Minnie sniffed. "But you tell her I'm here."

With shaking fingers, he parted the drape. When he looked at George, she smiled, and he responded in kind. Extending a hand, which he took in his, she met his gaze, and from that seemingly innocuous contact soothing warmth pervaded his flesh, eased his charged nerves, and erased the tension stiffening his spine.

In time with the constant tick tock of the wall clock, his pulse slowed, and he spoke to her in the mystical form of communication that was theirs, sharing secrets he'd never admitted to himself, much less anyone else, and she accepted him. In that instant, he bent his head and kissed her.

Joy shone in her expression, as she laughed. "All right. But can we stay at my place, because I have an en suite?"

~

Samhain, or Halloween, as most people called the holiday, marked the beginning of the Celtic New Year. It was a Sabbat to reflect on and honor ancestors, marking the dark time. In observance of the occasion, Haven Harbor held a huge ball at the Old Haven Mill Hotel. For the first time in her life, George had a date for the singular event, and she shivered with excitement. Just as quick, she sucked in a breath and gritted her teeth against the pain of her injuries.

"If you don't open this door in five minutes, I'm going to kick it down." Rafe pounded on the oak panel, and she giggled. "I mean it, George. I'm worried. You've been in there for over an hour."

"No need, doc." With one last check in the mirror, she twisted the lock, and he almost knocked her down, as he rushed into the bathroom. Balancing on her crutches, she bit her bottom lip. "What do you think?"

"Oh, babe." Framing her face, he kissed her—and kept kissing her. By the time he lifted his head, his hunger all but seduced her. "You're beautiful."

"The dress isn't too much?" The ebony, sleeveless *couture* gown, a gift from Rafe's mother, manifested every girl's dream, with a simple boat neck, a V-back, inverted pleats at the skirt, and a feather-embroidered lace overlay, fit to perfection and concealed her ankle cast. "And I don't look like a duck out of water?"

"You're stunning." With his teeth, he grazed the tip of her nose. "And if you weren't so banged up, I'd bend you over the counter and bang you right here."

"Okay." She hopped a little closer. "I'm game."

"No bouncy-bounce." He wagged a finger, as his energy broadcast concern for her welfare, and she couldn't resist him. "You've got bruised ribs. Trust me, the muscle contractions of an orgasm are the last thing you want or need."

"Says you." Skimming her palms across the starched front of his shirt, she pressed her lips to his. "I miss you, and I need to be close to you."

"Sweetheart, we share the same bed in the same house." In a flash, he reached behind her and pinched her butt. "And to my unmitigated frustration, you've taken the habit of wearing my boxers. In my book, that's pretty damned intimate."

"They're so comfortable." Wrapping her arms about his waist, she pressed her hips to his, and his breath hitched. "And my panties won't fit over the cast."

"So go without." He waggled his brows. "I prefer you like that."

"I would, if I thought it'd get me any action." A wave of emotion flooded her senses, as he retreated, and she couldn't quite grasp the meaning. "How'd the phone call go? Are your parents all right with your decision?"

"You know, it was interesting." With gentle movements, he guided her from the en suite and into what had quickly become their bedroom. "Mom seems totally fine with my accepting the position. In fact, she inquired after my intentions toward you, which was a little strange." Yet his inner musings conveyed certainty, regarding their relationship, and that shocked George. "Dad is still disappointed, but he'll get over it."

"Then it's settled?" Leaning against him, she passed him the crutches, which he propped against the wall. "As of Monday, you're the new Chief of ER Medicine at the hospital?"

"Yep." In one fell swoop, he swept her into his arms. "It's a done deal, baby." Moving slow and steady, to avoid jostling her, he carried her downstairs, and she took the opportunity to lick and suckle his ear. "Fuck. At this rate, I'm going to be hard until January."

"What about the car?" In her mind, she pictured a slew of possibilities. "I can straddle you, and we can prop my cast on the console."

"George, how many times do I have to remind you the cast is not the problem?" In the living room, he set her down and grabbed the second pair of crutches from the front closet. From the antique hall tree, he collected her coat, which he draped over her shoulders. As he secured the buttons, he grinned. "It's your ribs that concern me, but they're only fractured, which means you'll be good to go in about three to six weeks. I promise, you can ride me all you want after that."

"Spoilsport, and I'll hold you to that." She pouted and opened the front door. "Shall we head into town? We could take a room for the night. I've never had hotel sex."

"Easy, baby, and no, we won't." To say that Rafe had grown protective, since she came home from the hospital, was an understatement. The man fussed over everything, from breakfast, which he served in bed, to her baths, which he drew for her, to every seemingly insignificant detail, no matter how small, which he insisted on handling, and George loved him for it. "But how about you come to Manhattan with me, once you're healed, for a long weekend, because I need to put my apartment up for sale?" He raced ahead of her to unlock the car. "Be careful, or you might hurt yourself, and that would hurt me."

That was the one plea guaranteed to temper her actions, and she waited for him on the passenger side of the Mercedes, like a good girlfriend. With her seatbelt fastened, and the crutches stowed in the back, he navigated River Road and turned on Birch Street. After locating a space at the curb, near the main entrance, he parked and turned off the engine.

"So this is it?" He stared at the old hotel and exhaled. "The whole town has gathered, and there are more witches, inside?"

"They're all anxious to meet you, and you realize we're announcing ourselves as a couple, for everyone to see?" Based on her intuition, she surmised he'd rather curl up on the couch. "Nervous?"

"Not really." He sighed. "At least, not in the way you think."

"I don't understand." Confused by his sudden hesitance, she rested her palm to his forearm. "What's wrong?"

"Based on what you've told me, there are those who can read my thoughts. They can pick apart my past and dissect every idea that's entered my brain." Bowing his head, he twined his fingers with hers. "They'll know what I did. They'll know how I treated you, the morning you fell into the ravine."

"Yes, some will know, but that wasn't your fault. I was distracted, and I lost my footing. It was an accident." She squeezed his hand. "We are none of us perfect, Rafe. Trust me, given our history as witches, no one judges you here."

"I'm ashamed of how I behaved." As was his way, he pressed his lips to her knuckles. "Not a day goes by that I don't wish I could undo what happened, and I'll make it up to you, I swear."

"Hey, you're human, you have a right to be skeptical, and you're forgiven. It's over and done." Now she zeroed in on his desire, and what she read touched her everywhere. "It's okay. You don't have to say the words, because I hear you. In fact, there's never a point when I don't hear you. But that's why I wanted to take you hiking with me. When I'm alone with nature, everything goes quiet. There are no competing voices, shouting over each other for my attention, and I can center. I wanted to share that with you, and I will, when I'm able."

"Do you know how much I want to make love to you, right now?" With his thumb, he caressed her palm.

"Yes." Even in the dark of a new moon, the truth shone clear. Maybe more truth than he intended. "And I love you, too."

"Aw, babe." Stretched across the console, he cupped her cheek and kissed her. "I wanted to tell you, but then I figured it might shock you, and you're recovering from some serious injuries—"

"I'm fine, Rafe." George shrugged. "In fact, I'm better than fine. I'm happy."

"Me, too." With that, he slapped his thighs. "Okay, let's do it."

He exited the car, ran around to her side, opened the door, pulled her crutches from the backseat, and balanced her as she shifted to put her feet on the curb and stood. All the while, his energy cocooned her in an invisible but nonetheless protective embrace. When she swayed, he caught her, and revelatory emotion ignited the instant they touched.

"That's it." She snorted. "I'm blowing you as soon as we get home, because there's nothing wrong with my mouth, and you're about to explode."

"Well, if you insist." In the soft glow of lights from the hotel, she noted his boyish grin, which melted her heart. Then he thrust his chest and peered at her. "I do love you."

"I know." Step by step, they climbed the entrance stairs, and it was an ascendant journey in more ways than one. "So, is now a bad time to tell you I invited your parents to stay with us for Thanksgiving? Minnie is bringing the Plague."

EPILOGUE

October 1, 2017

"Ouch—shit." Rafe licked his burnt finger, snatched the potholder, and grabbed the hot handle of the cast-iron skillet. After scrambling the eggs, just as George liked them, he added a few tablespoons of her favorite hot sauce, some seasoned salt, and a fistful of shredded cheddar cheese, and mixed everything with a spatula. The microwave pinged, as he transferred the meal to a plate, so he draped a towel over the shallow basket he'd set on the bar, collected the steaming corn tortillas, which she preferred to flour, and arranged everything on a tray. The buzzer on the oven sounded, so he checked the cinnamon rolls. After icing the sweet treat she could never resist, he nodded once. "Wonder how she'll show her appreciation for this."

Smiling to himself, he recalled last night and their water games, after he had a hot tub installed on the back deck. To launch his scheme, he'd swapped shifts with another doctor, met the vendor that afternoon, rushed to the grocery store, raced to their sanctuary, and cooked dinner, soft meat tacos, her preference, and then she showed him how long she could hold her breath, as thanks for the meal. The ensuing naked and wet chase through their home ensured he would not achieve his primary goal, because she completely distracted him, so he resolved to try again. Still, the memorable evening would go down in the annals of their shared history, if only when he revealed his original plan.

Then he snapped his fingers. "Almost forgot the finishing touch."

From the pantry he retrieved a bud vase, filled it with water, and added it to his surprise. After pulling the scissors from a drawer, he walked to the kitchen table, picked a picture-perfect rose from the bouquet, one of many about the house, as his lady loved fresh flowers, trimmed the stem, and situated the bloom.

Standing back, he assessed his handiwork. "Not bad, Owen."

In the wake of George's injury, he'd moved into her place, in what was supposed to have been a temporary arrangement so he could take care of her. Of course, it became permanent, because he couldn't leave her. In fact, he couldn't see his future without her in it.

During those early precious months, Rafe had learned a lot about his witchy woman, about her unfailingly generous nature and kind heart, but he'd learned a lot more about himself, what he wanted, and how he pictured his ultimate fate. In short, everything revolved around George. While he enjoyed accompanying her on her litany of charitable visits, and there were many, he loved surprising her. Because, for all she did in the community, she never considered herself, and he aimed to correct that deficiency, as that was definitely a void he could and should fill. In light of her special gift, that was a difficult prospect, since she knew exactly what he wanted, so he figured out a way to fool her.

If he caught her first thing in the morning, before she fully woke, and he cleared his thoughts, he could succeed. It was with that objective he quietly entered their room—only to discover an empty bed.

"Good morning." Emerging from the en suite, with her hair in a ponytail, George tied her robe and stopped. "What's all this?"

"Take down your hair, drop the robe, and get back in bed." With a huff, he shuffled his feet. When she did as he asked, he frowned. "And lose the underwear, too."

"Yes, sir." Laughing, she wiggled out of her panties, which was enough to get him puffy, and eased between the sheets. "I should blow you more often."

"You already do, but I can never get enough of your mouth, baby." As she fluffed a pillow, he set the tray across her legs. "Comfortable?"

"Yes, but what's the occasion?" She tucked the covers beneath her arms. "It's not my birthday, and we aren't—"

In that instant, he realized she'd deciphered his motive. Almost at once, tears formed in her eyes, and she sobbed softly. "Rafe?"

"Hey, I wasn't trying to make you cry. In fact, I wanted to do this last night, but it fell by the wayside with your underwater Olympics." He perched on the edge of the mattress and draped an arm about her shoulders. "Come on, babe. I just want to make you happy and spoil you rotten for the rest of your life."

"I know, and I adore you for that." Sniffing, she cupped his cheek. "While I know what you want, and I'd bet you know my answer, I want you to say the words."

"I can do that." Drawing the velvet-covered box from his pocket, he knelt and clutched her hand. With his thumb, he flipped open the lid, revealing the simple two-carat diamond solitaire, in a platinum Tiffany setting, he'd selected just for her. "I hope you like it, because my mother helped me pick it out. Mary-George McBride, will you marry me?"

"Yes, of course, and the ring is beautiful." As he expected, she wept when he slipped the ring on her finger, and they shared a tender kiss. Then the mood changed as, with a yank, she snapped the waistband of his sweatpants. "Now get naked and join me, because I want to consummate our engagement."

"Food first, baby, although I like the way you think." After shedding his bottoms, he hopped in bed and scooted beside her. "I slaved over this meal, and there's plenty for two."

While he'd envisioned a leisurely romantic breakfast, which would end with even lengthier lovemaking, she shoved healthy bites into his mouth, interspersed with sweet kisses and gulps of coffee, and all but inhaled the cinnamon rolls.

Did she sense how much he wanted her? Did she comprehend the never-ending need?

"Hate to tell you this, but my mom wants to hold the wedding in Manhattan, at the Plaza." He dreaded sharing that bit of info.

"Minnie's going to want it here, in Haven Harbor, at the community center." George fed him a bite of cinnamon roll, and he licked her fingers. "And you know she'll insist on serving the Plague."

"The award-winning Perilously Perverted Peach Cobbler Plague, which now has four blue ribbons to its credit." He snickered. "We ought to outfit them in boxing gloves and put 'em in a ring. Damn, that's a fight I'd pay to see. While I love my mother, my money's on Minnie."

"She'd remind you that she intends to win a fifth cook off next weekend." With her fork, George scraped the last of the icing from her plate. "And my money's on Minnie, too, because she won't fight fair."

"Maybe we should elope." Considering the possibilities, he drained his mug. "How does Maui sound?"

"That might be the safest, not to mention

sanest, option. All right, I can't wait anymore." Nuzzling his neck, she nipped his skin. "I want you."

Without a word, he set the tray on the floor and returned to his witch. As usual, she made the first move, working his erection, and he figured he would follow her aggressive lead, as she held his stare and smiled her feminine smile. To his amazement, she kissed him, pulled away, threw her pillow aside, and reclined. He should have known better, because she understood what he wanted to do for her, so she surrendered.

As Rafe rolled atop her and spread her thighs, he framed her face. For a while, he simply gazed into her beautiful blue eyes, speaking to her in her unique language. In his focused thoughts, he told her what she meant to him, what she did for him, and what he wanted for their future. Despite his instincts to plow, and the growing hunger, he wanted to take his time with the woman who would be his wife. "I love you, George."

"I know you do." Wrapping her legs about his waist, she tilted her hips in welcome but made no other move. "Because I love you, too. And that's no magick."

ABOUT BARBARA DEVLIN

Bestselling, Amazon All-Star author Barbara Devlin was born a storyteller, but it was a weeklong vacation to Bethany Beach, DE that forever changed her life. The little house her parents rented had a collection of books by Kathleen Woodiwiss, which exposed Barbara to the world of romance, and Shanna remains a personal favorite. Barbara writes heartfelt historical romances that feature flawed heroes who may know how to seduce a woman but know nothing of marriage. And she prefers feisty but smart heroines who sometimes save the hero, before they find their happily ever after. Barbara earned an MA in English and continued a course of study for a Doctorate in Literature and Rhetoric. She happily considered herself an exceedingly eccentric English professor, until success in Indie publishing lured her into writing, full-time, featuring her fictional knighthood, the Brethren of the Coast.

Connect with Barbara Devlin at BarbaraDevlin.com, where you can sign up for her newsletter, The Knightly News.
Facebook:
https://www.facebook.com/BarbaraDevlinAuthor
Twitter: @barbara_devlin

TITLES BY BARBARA DEVLIN

BRETHREN OF THE COAST
Enter the Brethren
My Lady, the Spy
The Most Unlikely Lady
One-Knight Stand
Captain of Her Heart
The Lucky One
Love with an Improper Stranger
To Catch a Fallen Spy
The Duke Wears Nada

Loving Lieutenant Douglas: A Brethren of the Coast
Novella
Hold Me, Thrill Me, Kiss Me: A Brethren of the Coast
Novella

BRETHREN ORIGINS
Arucard
Demetrius
Aristide

PIRATES OF THE COAST
The Black Morass

KATHRYN LE VEQUE'S KINDLE WORLD OF DE
WOLFE PACK
Lone Wolfe
The Big Bad De Wolfe